Returning Back
& Other Short Stories

By

Susan Brice

Returning Back & other short stories

© 2015 Susan Brice

Email: susan.brice.englishtutor@gmail.com

www.lakestay.co.uk/susanbrice

Dedicated to all those who
suffer from 'invisible' illness.

*(& with many thanks to:
Richard B, Carol, Ali,
Jacqueline, Ray & Dan.)*

Foreword

2014 was the year in which reality went on the blink for me: everything changed. Latterly things have started to settle down though the journey of self-discovery will last for always. Writing has helped me to explore – 'stuff'… So these stories are something of a lucky dip into life's bran tub. Or as King Lear puts it: "Let me not be mad"… Least ways, dear reader, try not to be mad with me: these are the children of my imaginings.

Susan Brice
Maryport 2015

Index

1. Taking The First Step

The suggestion is made: 'Perhaps you might like to think about...' My instant reaction, 'No, I don't think so, not at the moment.' Then the onrush of thoughts. I walk into the dawning day as the black night gives way to the weak winter light, dark clouds swirl above my head, the beach is bleak, the sea a still and steely grey. My dog is at my side, tugging eagerly at his lead, he presses forward, wants to get ahead. I observe his red brown glee as he leaps towards the water and rushes into the deeps.

Oh to be a dog, to know only the kindness of humans: to be fed, watered, cared for loved. All this unconditional. This is how I see my dog, more child than animal: compensation for...? No, I am not going to unburden my soul: that is for my confessor. This is me in abstract: sifting for self.

What is being? To be is to exist. What does my dog know of being? Sometimes in the early hours of the morning he feels cold and begs to share the warmth of our bed. He sleeps in the kitchen. He has a comfortable bed filled with blankets of different kinds: a large off-white linen one patterned with raised squares and zigzags; a purple polyester leopard print throw, bought as a bargain from a 'Pound Shop'; a thick woollen piece of cloth, formerly a the cover of a bobbin rocking chair, multi-coloured, now shrunk to a lump through repeated washing; and finally, the small, brown square – a piece of the blanket upon which he was born. Does this brown square mean a thing to him? The smells of birth, mother and doggy siblings are long gone from his memory: we are his family now.

He met his mother, about a year ago. She was smaller than I remembered, blacker - smoother haired. He is a good six inches taller than she; his fur is a scruffy mess, sticking out all over the place making him look like a shaggy teddy bear. She sniffed cautiously at his rear end, he rewarded her by barking, viciously, warningly, would have taken out her throat had we not been there to restrain. What were they saying to each other? He, perhaps, "You let them take me, I hate you." She, responding, "I had no choice, all my pups were taken." You say to yourself, this woman anthropomorphises: she lays her feelings of guilt upon the bitch.

The dog wades, splashes, rolls in the sea, he courses rapidly along the water, up to his knees. He dashes in and out, sometimes shaking, sometimes rolling, always smiling. He has a proper doggy smile, ingenuous, willing to please. I watch a flight of Oyster Catchers as they range across the cloudy sky, dodging among small, weak beams of light. The light is breaking through the darkness, a feeble attempt to dispel the gloom which permeates the frigid atmosphere. They squeal and wheel, call and cackle. Was it always so? These birds flying here, feeding on unlucky crustaceans, day long. Did they wheel and call at the beginning of time before man was? I look at the birds, the rocky sand, the waves, they were here before I was, they will be here when I am not: long after the demise of the last human being. They were before the first human being took his first steps.

First Steps: that's what they call it, this process of beginning to search for self. No stigma, no need to hide what you are – even though you may be unsure of this yourself - even though self seems to be the centre of all that you do not want to confront.

I ponder the dog, the sea, the beach, the birds, the morning. I am in mourning, grieving for the child, the woman, the mother. Me. I need to speak to the past: I need the past to speak to me. I need the past to explain the gaps, the things I do not, did not understand. The only longing I have now, at this present moment is that I would like not to exist. Not a cry for help, not a cry at all – in fact the opposite. Paradoxically, I am asking you not to notice me, not to see me not to wonder whether I am waving or drowning: I am doing neither.

If I could just, become one with this moment. Cease my corporeal existence, become a non-being, melt away: that is what I would do. It feels far too complicated to continue and I lack the energy which would lead me to snuff out my own life: I have lost the will to be, I have lost the will to not be. I want to fade into un-being. But of course you can't un-be, whilst still breathing, you are, I am. But what am I?

I call the bounding dog back to my side, he shakes his wet body and sprinkles me with droplets of cold, cold water. I shiver. We walk on, the breeze is getting up and causing an icy blast to penetrate my many layers of clothing.

"You see," I say to the dog as we perambulate the shore, "You see, I would like you to help me to assemble the pieces. You have no human sensibilities, I can tell you what is in my heart: you will not judge me, you will not tell." I see the problem, I need to be absolved of guilt, I need forgiveness but cannot see from whence it could come. Companion, good listener, my furry friend you may be but you, dear boy cannot give me any kind of absolution.

We walk away from the beach, along the grassy tracks and waste lands where, in spring the larks ascend, singing for sheer joy of being. I hear the strains of violin, of bird song, those shivery opening notes, 'Laah, la,la, laah; La, la, laah, la, laah…' The bliss of music and nature combined, the rhythms that run through life. I recall this on this morning, the joy of the skylark, the joy of creation as spring rises at the heart of nature. Where can I find my Spring? Where can I, this dried up bulb of failed potential: where can I find the will to germinate, to throw up tentative new shoots?

We crown the slope and look across the Firth to Scotland. On the horizon, the shoreline curves to infinity, I cannot see round the farthest curve, I cannot see what is over the highest mountain. A thin misty shroud wafts and lingers in this early morning. I remark upon this stillness

to the dog, he sniffs around a piece of low grass. The sniff is thoughtful, pee-mail from another dog, or several. He nods his head in appreciation, then proceeds to lift his leg and leave a message for the next passing canine. Message left, he walks on. The grass is thin, there are patches of palest green, some mossy brown and some, but very little, deep, deep green. By the end of spring the grass will be waist high, a spectrum of greens, a corny-yellow. But now, the earth is laid bare, almost but not quite.
("Perhaps you might like to think about..."
"No, I don't think so, not at the moment...")

As we ascend to the harbour, the tide has risen and covered the basin almost up to the edge of the road. Fishing boats bob precariously at the road's edge, seemingly wanting to escape the waves and sail into the town. The dog stops and looks, he sits on his hindquarters, refusing to move.

The thing I love about this dog is that he believes he is the Harbour Master: he notes activities and questions changes, "What," his little doggy face says, "is going on here? No one asked me, I did not order it." He begins to growl and then to bark, this change is not to his liking. My dog knows every inch of the harbour. He knows where the fishing nets lie, where the plastic fish boxes are piled: he has a sense of the order of things, the order of being on the harbour. Something new, alien or out of place is commented upon. Today it is the height of the tide. One day we came walking after a very heavy wind, about 20 yards ahead of us lay a jagged piece of wood, it was tarry and very black. The dog pulled up short, alarmed. He stood to attention, his nose and tail showing the merest flicker. "Stop! Stop right there, you need to be protected and I small dog, big heart, will protect you." Cautiously he went up to the wood, scented the air, waited. "Salty, tarry" said his nose, "hmm." He could afford to move a little closer. He lowered himself on his haunches, stretched his front paws out and crept towards the thing. He pounced, then backed off as if checking the reaction he might get. He gave a little bark, when the wood did not move, he stood boldly on all four legs and walked straight to it, pawing it gently at first and then more vigorously, the wood flipped, the dog bounced back, pawed the ground went in for the kill. He nudged the wood over the quayside, dusted his paws together, told me I was now safe to proceed. I love my dog, he makes me laugh, he keeps me safe.

I am safe with my dog – so that must count as a 'Be', I AM conjugated from the verb 'To be.' So this part of me is not a puzzle at all, I can make a statement to myself, I am the owner of this dog. Some might say I am the mother of this dog: this does not make me a bitch.

Two columns then, one headed I AM… and the other I AM NOT… Then a neat line under each heading. Mentally I complete the first column: I am the owner of this dog;I follow suit with the second column: I am not a bitch. That actually feels good as I think-write it,something of note, something I can confirm, have evidence for.

The dog senses that my mind is wandering, we dawdle, he sniffs and scents, I drift.

The morning has now been fully born into the day. It is a dim day, I look up to the heavens and search for rays of light, those tiny beams which prove that we are not alone in the universe. A Payne's Grey sky with few breaks in the floating clouds. And I see them there, almost imperceptible, little promises of light behind. The Light of the World comes to mind, Holman Hunt's revelatory vision of Christ. He stands clothed about with darkness, all about him seems dead, the trees and landscape in winter mode, there is an elderly gate, firmly closed and He is knocking. He is the bringer of light, a lantern beaming in his other hand, a nimbus radiating from his head. "Behold," he says, "I stand at the gate and knock…" Hunt was portraying the infinitely closed human mind. Is my mind closed? Is my mind beyond reach of help? ("Perhaps you might like to think about…")

The dog and I, now walking at a slow but unified pace, approach the steps, which lead to home. I count the first set of six up to the first concrete landing. Teardrops of rain begin to fall, the dog shakes them away, I wish for wipers on my spectacles, the way ahead is fuzzy. Seeing, stepping, being – they are all hazardous at this moment: I could fall on these steps, the dog could trip me. I could fall over my own feet.

The sky is now indigo, not one ray of light is seeping through the darkness. The morning has reverted to night. My mood hovers as we cross the road and head for home: up or down? And then it occurs to me that this is the choice, this is the chance to find out who me is, who I be, who be I? I have 'liked to think about...'.

The dog waits as I unlock the front door, I loose his leash, he bounds into the kitchen in search of a drink. I steady myself as I remove first waterproof jacket, then waterproof trousers, thick fleece, scarf and woolly hat. There are so many layers before I reach me. I need a drink too - coffee, bitter and black. The kettle heats, the water pours onto the grounds and seeps slowly through the filter: I pour the hot liquid into a bowl shaped mug and cradle it in my hands. The dog has had his fill of water, he is slumped in his bed, toasting his nose on the bars of the grate.

Still sipping at my coffee, I take the phone in hand and dial the number: I have thought about, I am taking those first steps.

(**There are times in life when reality goes on the blink – this happened to me. Dan, my G.P suggested that I call First Step which is part of NHS Cumbria Mental Health Service. To confront yourself with the idea that you are not in the best of mental health is difficult.)

2. Dressing Down

It had been one of those worse than usual bad-hair days, the awfulness had gathered pace. The morning was dark, miserable and wintery, the air outside her duvet was freezer level: bed seemed like a nice place to be. If only she'd stayed there…

Valerie was a teacher at a local secondary school; not going to work, except in extreme circumstances, was simply not an option. She groped for the light-switch, nothing happened, she looked at her alarm clock, it was dead; truth dawned. It was a bloody power cut! Muttering she picked her way carefully from beneath the bedclothes and groped about for her watch, the time was… the time was… she screwed up her eyes and tried to focus, the time was… "Bloody hell! I'm late!" she shouted, groping in the pitch darkness for the first clothes that came to hand and then panicking her way through rush hour traffic to the school steps.

School itself was bathed in a warm glow of electric light, so no chance of a closure today then, thought Valerie as she battled her way up the steps with a bag full of marked books. She dumped the bag on the nearest desk, hurriedly switched on the computer whilst trying simultaneously to engage with lost ties, sick notes, and whines. Smaller than the average Year 7, poor Stanley was in tears: his lunch had been pinched the previous day and his Mam was that mad - she threatened to belt him for not standing up for himself. The logic of the threat escaped Valerie, the child's need for comfort did not. The tutor group *('Vertical Tutoring': blend the different year groups together for better socialisation)* let themselves into her room, sitting steadfastly in their peer groups - she'd given up trying to force them to socialise with each other. She cast an eye around the room in search of a kinder, older child who might be a buddy to Stanley but feared there was no candidate for this role. As the students came in, they gave her some odd looks, but said nothing. Except of course for, Year 9 Grace, who always had to express an opinion, "You look nice today, Miss", the bland remark was accompanied by an 'I-mean-the-opposite' smirk.

Throughout the morning she received further curious glances from staff and students. No one actually said anything but when she went into the canteen to collect her morning snack, she distinctly heard a mutter from the gaggle of kids she'd queue jumped: a suspicious ill-suppressed giggle rippled on the air.

Children, *'young adults'*, she knew could be hard on their elders if you gave them a chance, Valerie never had given them a chance: her over-the-glasses-stare could floor a child at twenty paces. It was not until the Head stopped her in the corridor and asked her, pointedly, if she felt quite well, that 'Miss' decided she'd better take a more careful look at herself. However, this was before the break-time incident during which Tom Bullock (probably descended from the china shop variety) misdirected a fast flying ball. What a mouthful she gave him as she confiscated the ball. The damage was done though: she now sported a shining black eye.

She went into the loo to clean up and took a glance in the long mirror: the image she presented was startling. She surveyed the damage. Fortunately, in spite of the black eye, her hair was in its usual neat trim; this pleased her if nothing else did. On a normal, 'un-bad-hair day', she dressed soberly – black tights, pristine white blouse, black jacket and black skirt- sometimes if she was in a jocular mood she would add a gaily coloured scarf but this was the extent of her daring. The impenetrability of this disguise helped her daily performance as TEACHER. But this was, as you may recall, a bad, bad hair day and Valerie had dressed in the dark, in a hurry.

You may wonder how it was that a normally, smart professional woman came to be so untypically dressed. The thing was, that her sister had left a pile of chucked out clothes for her to sort through the previous evening. Val *(her out of school name)* had sorted the clothes into three piles: Maybe, Definitely Not and Yes. She had also laid out her clothes for the morning but somewhere along the line, in the pitch darkness things had become confused. Yes, she had had one or two glasses of Prosecco, pleasant cold and fizzy but it hadn't gone to her head? Really, no, surely not? With mounting horror, she gazed at her reflection.

She was wearing a vermillion sunrise shirt, complete with insane merry-go-round appliqué in gaudy felt colours. The jacket, cropped to the waist (how could she not have noticed even in the dark?) was a turbulent orange, which disagreed viciously with the shirt. At best it was avant-garde at worst, it made her feel she wanted to vomit. The skirt was quite tame by comparison, a faux kilt affair in red tartan complete with blanket pin. Each of her legs took care to look especially uncoordinated – the tights she had put on were a vivid purple, which would not have been so bad had it not been for the pattern of circus clowns with red gashes for mouths dancing lazily up her calves and knees. To complete the chaotic picture, the shoes were odd. On one foot she wore a sequined pink slip-on and on the other, a ballet pump in acid green. Valerie cussed silently to herself, her sister's taste in clothing was far from mainstream, but this combination? What to do?

She could have asked to go home, saying she felt unwell, or maybe phone the switchboard and say there was a bomb in the school – now that was a thought, they'd all get sent home for the afternoon while the police searched the building. Trouble was they'd probably trace the phone call and find out that she was the culprit. No, there was only one way to deal with this, shoulders back, head high this was her choice and no one, but no one was allowed to comment. In the mirror she brushed off the lapels of her jacket, practised her hardest stare, smoothed the skirt, muttered "Scotts wha hae..." or something similar and marched back to her classroom with quiet determination.

The rest of the morning was spent tackling the unpleasant proclivities of the Roman invaders combined with her steeliest of steel glances. By the time she reached her lunch break, she was quite pleased with the way she had frozen out her situation with both staff and students. A rather forward Newly Qualified Teacher had smiled and said, 'off to a rehearsal?' In response she had given him a steely stare, pursed her lips and said coldly 'Don't be impertinent'. He had withered and walked away muttering something about the weather forecast for the weekend. It has to be said though that this stance had been hard work and she felt really hungry. Today was not a day, Valerie thought to herself, for a baguette from the school canteen; today was a day for something high quality in the junk food department. She got into her car and drove to the shops, parking neatly beside a green land-cruiser.

Lunch hour, actually being forty minutes, of which ten had already passed, Valerie felt the pressure of time at her heels and raced into 'Hit and Run' the local fast food joint. Exactly three minutes later she rushed out with a steadily warming paper carrier bag. At that point a young woman stepped neatly in front of her and asked if she'd mind answering a few questions for a survey? The questions seemed innocuous enough – what she liked to eat, favourite colours and so forth: and as Val noticed the time ticking on, she agreed to a photo, it could do no harm. Then she rushed away thinking little more about it. As she arrived at her car, she noticed the land-cruiser had gone, taking part of her wing mirror with it: she did not even have time to curse, let alone eat the food she so longed to comfort herself with.

Later that day, following a sixty-minute phone call to Vic (her sister) where she detailed her woes, she changed into leggings and a baggy top. In the fridge she found the almost empty bottle of Prosecco, had the good grace to blush a little, poured out the remains and reheated the thoroughly unhealthy, high fat, high salt, no Five A Day meal for two from 'Hit and Run'. She thought over the course of this very irritating day. Her mind went back to the wing mirror – that would have to be dealt with, better phone the garage in the morning; then she thought about the survey woman. What had she said? Something about make-over, healthy eating and, surely not, but yes, and contact details… Oh hell, Val thought, there'll be a few unsolicited phone calls now offering me goodness knows what.

On the point of opening her emergency bottle of Prosecco prior to settling down to that lovely family game of 'marking 9Cs school books', the phone rang. "Is that Valerie?" enquired an unknown voice. She responded in the affirmative: "Hi, Val darling, you'll know me I'm sure from the telly box?" A vague memory stirred in her brain, was it that twit who did some quiz show? No she shifted her brain further into gear, no, no it was…"Yes darling, it's me – Arty Aardvark…*SOS MY Clothes*." He paused to hear her swoon, Valerie managed a strangled sigh: was this some kind of joke?

As it happened, it was not a joke and somehow, after a half-hour chat Val found that she had agreed to take part in Arty's *'Reality T.V. Show.'* Had she been in her right mind, Val would have said a very firm no, but Arty was persuasive and told her that out of "simply hundreds of possibles, sweetheart" she had been chosen. 'Chosen' that word had an irresistible ring to it and sod it, she never had had a proposition like this before. But how on earth would she live down Arty's prying eyes – his catch line *'AA the fourth emergency service – always there to save you from yourself'*.

The following Saturday a confirmatory email plopped into her inbox, there were dates, times AND the information that she would need an entire week away from the chalk-face at the T.V. company's expense. Ha, she thought, there's the get out, Mr BIG would never agree to that! Curiously enough, he did… "Valerie, what an innovator you are, it'll be such good publicity for the school, they'll want to run some kind of feature in the local press and we can link it all in with Textiles, Miss Furbellow will love it!" She was, in effect, hoist on her own high heels, quite defenceless in the face of BIG's publicity hungry nature.

Valerie did try to point out to the star struck Head that this was not University Challenge, Eggheads or even Pointless, but he simply waved her away saying it would be much more embarrassing to have her general knowledge tested and found wanting. Open mouthed at this response, Valerie left his office in a rumble of defiant thunder. Damn it all, she might be 'discovered' who knew what programmes the talent scouts tuned into? It had always been her secret ambition to star as Elinor Glyn, complete with tiger skin.

Taking time out of the classroom for a day requires preparation, taking time out of the classroom for an entire week requires so much preparation that many teachers often question whether the 'out' time meets the value of 'in' time: all time out is weighed extremely carefully. Valerie had all this to do alongside the usual every day marking and preparation as well as the odd extra after school meeting ('attendance-is-not-required-but-if-you-ain't-there-your-absence-will-noted'). She found herself burning not only midnight oil but some of the early morning variety as well just to make sure she was up to speed for her *Grand Week Out* as MR BIG kept referring to it. Her request for absence had turned into a massive, massive favour which only he could grant and he wanted to be certain that she was fully aware of his munificence. Her gratitude was limited based on the fact that it would not cost the school a penny and she had all but completed the work for her classes in advance.

So it was that she packed her bags and headed for the hotel where the next episode of *'S.O.S. My Clothes'* was to be filmed. She was dressed casually, her mufti consisting of a russet brown tunic top over a pair of skinny jeans. She hummed to herself as she left the train, the day was sunny, there was not a cloud, a stupid Head or a troublesome child on the horizon – the latter two not for an entire week, what could go wrong?

At the hotel, the researcher (Flamenco Deans), who had interviewed Val in the street, met her with gloomy face. 'Did she, by any chance, have the clothes she had been wearing 'that day' in her bag?' 'Why no,' Val responded, are they required?' Required! Arty had been quite specific about her clothing. He had selected her from simply ZILLIONS of possibles, did Val not understand that it was her look Arty was after?

Fortunately Val had not had a chance to deposit the offending outfit at her nearest charity shop: it was lying, bagged up to avoid further mix ups, in the bottom of her wardrobe. Flamenco's face relaxed into a relieved smile, what were they waiting for then? Quickly, quickly, a taxi back to Val's flat and all would be well.

Arty Aardvark (call me Arty Darling) met Val and three other people at lunch. He swooped down on the three of them, hugging them and air kissing them as though they were long lost relatives raised from the dead. Judging by the way each of them was dressed, they probably were. Arty Darling just couldn't WAIT (upward inflection on the word wait as he spat it out) to get to know them. Flamenco has done him proud in finding us, he is soooooo delighted and Flamenco will be in for a bonus, so she is grinning like a peach.

The four victims rose after their pleasant lunch with Arty, little suspecting the humiliation which lay in store for them. Everywhere they went, they were accompanied by the recording crew, Flamenco, and supernumery bodies whose function it was hard to make out. Words like 'Darling', 'Sweetie', 'Precious' were flung about with all the subtlety of confetti, always with that irritating upward inflection. To Val's annoyance, she found she caught the style and could not help using it too.

Her 'companions' for the week looked as at sea as she felt, terrified of what they'd let themselves in for and yet quite caught up by the excitement of it all. Mavis a 45-

year-old dental receptionist was really sweet; Val liked her gentle voice and quiet manner. She had been caught out, like Val, on a bad hair day. "I was just nipping out to the supermarket early one Saturday at a time when no right minded person would be up and about when Flamenco jumped out on me: I was quite startled!" Mavis was a large lady; she was wearing a multi-patterned, multi-coloured caftan which looked as though it had been made from an old duvet cover. Her feet were encased in a pair of furry, pink ankle boots over the tops of which her somewhat fat ankles bulged ungraciously.

Matthew (who Arty insists on calling Matty Sweetheart) has a fixed cheesy grin and it's difficult to get him to do more than nod or 'hummmm' in reply to anything. The 'hummmmms' vary in length at times sound a little like a squeak. Matty Sweetheart is shy, nervous and obviously afraid of what Arty is going to reveal about him. He is about 60, a retired scaffolder. At a glance it appears that he has not updated his wardrobe since Peter Wingard was on the telly. He is wearing a lurid, acid green caftan, with purple bell-bottoms and has a drooping moustache complemented with heavy gold jewellery. Val was unsure what to make of him but as the week progressed and the four of them got to know each other better, she discovered Matthew had a wicked sense of humour when not feeling attacked.

Finally there was Robert, 28: sturdy bank manager type of person in official bank manager type gear right down to the furled umbrella, waistcoat – although there was no sign of a bowler hat. He was very vocal, well-spoken and something in the city (how predictable). Flamenco had leapt on him when he went to get himself a bite to eat from a vegan take-away.

Then the humiliation begins. Arty announces that he wants them all to change from within. He talks about the inner-self, the real 'you' and the outer- self, watched over by guardian angels, wafted on a breeze, unsure, afraid. Apparently all four of them had 'spoken' to

Flamenco, calling out loudly 'Help me find true self'. Val thought hard but could not remember communicating anything of the sort. Arty informs them that they will face a rigorous re-programming using his own, unique techniques. "Darlings, I'll be mucking about with your make-up, doing the dirty on your diets," he shakes a finger at Val, "No more take-aways for you my girl! Aaand I'll be rifling through your drawers... OOH Watch it sailor," he smirks at Matty with a cheeky grin.

As it turned out the week was fun if excruciatingly embarrassing in places. They were pushed and pummelled, made to meditate despite the uncontrollable desire each of them had to giggle loudly, and were asked searching questions about what they ate and why. Complete hair restyling was the order of the day, fashion consultants brought in by Arty made decisions without reference to his new friends: these decisions were made based on auras, birth signs and for some strange reason, their reaction to a sheet of ink blots. This latter, Val concluded, was a mere cherry on the top of the whole flimsy cake but knew it would be lapped up by the viewers – S.O.S. Your Wardrobe drew almost the same audience as Coronation Street.

By the end of the week, Val had made three firm friends, in particular Matthew (she couldn't call him Matty) the ex-scaffolder. The four of them agreed to get together at Mavis's place to watch the outcome when it was broadcast. They had buckets of popcorn to hand, several bottles of Chilean wine and had ordered a take-away for afters.

They sat and watched, open mouthed as the show unfolded, at points Matthew hid his face behind a cushion, Robert exclaimed loudly using various expletives, Mavis shook with laughter and Val's eyes opened so wildly they were in danger of popping. It's hard to believe that throughout the recording, they are all grinning whilst Arty and his gang made prats of them all. Why, they wondered, were they grinning? Why, they wondered, hadn't they told Arty to stick his outlandish ideas and walked out?

Mavis is condemned for her weight, Arty calls her a 'Regular fatty bum-bums' much to the amusement of the studio audience. In the sequence where he looks in Mavis's wardrobe, he holds up a pair of 'big-knickers' wonders if they could be used as a marquee and pulls 'you-know-what' faces as the audience rock with the hilarity of it all. Mavis is 're-born', S.O.S rescued her from herself with a lettuce leaf diet plan and a Wonder-Woman-Body-Shaper – admittedly she did look classy in her 'Big & Beautiful' trouser suit with long length jacket and stylish scarf, muted autumn tones with a hint of winter sun but none of them were convinced by the champagne pink streaks in her newly cropped hair. 'Thank goodness it's begun to grow out,' Mavis muttered. By the time the show went out, she'd discarded the Wonder-Woman-Body-Shaper – preferring the gentle art of breathing - but had stuck to the diet plan. "Now that,' she informed the others, I did find useful."

Matthew confessed to the company assembled on the sofa that he'd been caught by Flamenco on his way back from a 60's night – the moustache had always been his pride and joy. Matthew's on screen self listens as Arty goes through his wardrobe and flings out, outfit after outfit – each one set in a 60s/70s time-warp. "Saving it all up for Armageddon were you Matty lad?" In fact, Matthew had more than one wardrobe but Arty wasn't even prepared to look elsewhere and hit on the 'antiques' he described them as perfect fly-on-the-wall stuff for the show. As was Matthew's secret stock of Haribos, which Arty found, stashed in a tin under the stairs. "Get this," says Arty looking straight into the camera, "I'd like to bet he munches on these behind closed curtains…" a giggle from the audience. Arty pushes it a bit more, "Are you Matty, are you a secret muncher? Come on confess!" with each word, he nudges Matthew suggestively. The Haribos are in fact treats left over from a previous visit by grandchildren but this explanation has been edited out and Matthew simply looks red and guilty as hell when confronted thus. Matthew explains to his new mates, "I was getting so fed up at that point it took me all my time to stop myself from thumping him... that constant bloody pawing." They all agreed that work on the show had been far too touchy feely for their tastes, but not one of them had had the moral courage to ask Arty to stop. The audience look on in awed silence as Arty hands Matthew a lighter and eggs him on to set light to the bell-bottoms: they flare up and a stage hand rushes on with an extinguisher. The applause goes on for over a minute and looks like it might turn into a standing ovation. But an ovation for whom? The curtains swish back and the new Matty steps out and at this point, the audience does rise to its feet. He's wearing a sharp, midnight blue suit with crisp white shirt – one button undone at the neck, red white and blue striped tie slantwise – his hair has been messed up into a Rod Stewart style and his shoes are so shiny they reflect the studio lights. No doubt about it, Matty the retired scaffolder looks fantastic, a new, new man indeed... "But just not you," commented Val as they watched, "I think I like you better in your green polo shirt and chinos."

In direct contrast, it seemed that Arty thought 'something in the city' Robert was just too straight laced to be believed. "You're 28 lad, old age will come on you soon enough. A bit afraid of pulling eh?" yet again Arty winked into the camera lens, taking the audience with him whilst excluding Robert. "Robbie, my boy, time to loosen up the looks." And Robert was loosened up. His wardrobe had been condemned for containing too many sober suits, monochrome shirts and no evidence of gym-wear. "Tell me truthfully, Robert sweetheart, you are a stranger to exercise aren't you, aren't you." Arty fills up with the horror of it all. Again, the point at which Robert explains that he cycles a round trip of 20 miles to work each day, is cut from the final show and Arty's implication that Robert is a 6 stone weakling who gets sand kicked in his face is upheld before the shocked studio audience. Robert is taken to Freddy the Fork-Full-Friend who suggests that his vegan diet is somewhat restricted and that there should more seaweed, carbs and a bowl of dried Oak Leaves each week to calm his nervous aura. Robert nods knowingly at all of this while thinking 'what a dick-head'. His subsequent transformation – massaged and mutated by a facial with judicious application of 'Man-C-Up' a product for look-savvy men aged under 30. He looked bronzed and beefed up by the treatment, his skinniness had given way to a lean hungry look, the distressed jeans and loose shirt complimented the blonde streaks which brightened up his hair. "I reckon," said Robert, "I got away with the least collateral damage." Mavis responded, "Well you would do – you're the baby of the group." Robert promptly bashed her with a pillow.

Finally as Arty hummed the tune, *'An Apple For the Teacher,'* Val made her appearance. "Val, ladies and gents, Val was THE ONE S.O.S. My Clothes KNEW, just KNEW they could do the most for." His voice dropped to a soft confidential whisper, "Imagine, this, the Val we found on the streets teaching the up and coming generation..." A massive picture of Val on her bad-hair day filled the screen. "I should think the kids needed therapy after being locked in with this loony-lady for 50 minutes." Val sat, speechless, had she really let him get away with that? The answer was yes, but not with the crack about the cross-eyed teacher being unable to control her pupils and happily her angry put down had been edited out. Arty listed Val's offences in all areas relating to her dress code and eating habits. Of the four participants, Val had been the one subject to the widest range of alternative therapies, the more outlandish the better. She had been covered from head to foot in mud, raised from the floor by the single finger of a fakir. Her angel had been described in minute detail; apparently it was her late Aunt Maud (unknown to Val until this point) who had guided Flamenco to bring her deliverance through Arty's good offices. The four of them gasped as Val's final form was revealed to an ecstatic audience: Her telly-self stepped out onto the stage. Her hair had been blunt cut by an intense-faced young hopeful, no streaks, no gimmicks just her grey-white hair made to shimmer, her face was framed, the cut softened the lines. She was clothed in a deep purple wrap-over with modest décolletage; a black belt studded with 'gold' gems and on her feet was a pair of strappy, black, wedge-heeled sandals. "You've gotta admit," swooned Matthew, "You do look stunning girl." Somehow during the broadcast, the two had moved closer together. And she did admit it, Val did look good.

On reflection, it had been a crazy but enjoyable fantasy week which had taken Val and the others out of the humdrum into the manic. Not one of them regretted anything, except perhaps not assassinating Arty or feeding Flamenco to a passing crocodile. Val smiled at the memory, at school 'Mr Big' had congratulated her on a wonderful performance and trusted they would see more of her artistic self from now on. The kids rushed into her classes, eager to share the generally held view that Val had been 'AWESOME' even her colleagues did not grudge her her fifteen minutes of fame. Best of all though, Val had been contacted by a casting company – might she be interested in the part of Elinor Glyn *(the lady who sinned on a tiger skin)* in a new biopic? Her features were just ideal...

3. Let's Get Lost

Prologue

Chet Baker sings in the background, a voice redolent with the smell and sound of toasting coffee beans. "Let's get lost..." he all but whispers to me and I think, 'thanks Chet, maybe I just will.'

Introducing myself is somewhat complex, so please bear with me. I think it's best to explain in terms of three: whoops – you think I think I'm the Deity? Good grief no, just one of His (or probably Her) creations. The three works like this: I have a right side of my head, a sort good cop or maybe angel side and a left side of my head – bad cop/devil etc. And then there is me, caught in the middle. In order to untangle this tricky little knot, perhaps I need to give each of the three parts a name: (yes, three in one and one in three but please bear in mind that I do not believe I am GOD, that would be far too silly).

I was really thinking it through this morning on my walk with the dog, how to really explain, how to make you understand. I said to myself: well, just call your selves 'Good Cop/Bad Cop' or maybe give your selves more feminine names: Angelica and Devilla. Problem is that is far too simple and besides, what do I call 'me'? This is because, sometimes, in fact, quite often, I or Me (a name I didn't call myself) feels a bit like piggy in the middle to the other two. And I don't want to use my ACTUAL birth certificate name a)because I'm not that keen on it and b) because it's only one dimension. If I call 'me' by my name in this tale, you'll simply see the 'me' that you perceive...

(That is if you know me, it's probably simpler to ask all those who DO know me to exit the tale at this stage as you may find it will make your head explode. Exploding heads?! Uh, oh, how much would that cost me in legal fees? So please take this parenthesis as a disclaimer on my part. Something along the lines of: Reader, I warned you.)

...It was then that I began to consider King Lear. That dusty, confused old pal of Mr. S *(or Mr B if you prefer, so even this is not straight forward)* and I thought perhaps I could explain myself in terms of King Lear. So at this point, enter stage left, right and centre – Leah.

Good Cop becomes 'Cordelia', misguided, loving daughter, selfless, kind and good. There she is as part of my eternal triangle. She speaks kindly, listens nicely and believes the best of everyone, raises money for charity, goes the extra mile and is exceptionally kind to and aware of all of creation, especially dogs. Yes, there she is, decent little Cordelia, the one so many people know and think is Leah. It is she who aches for the state of every part of humanity, who feels responsible for everything from the broken butterfly wing, to the war in any particular part of the world, to famine, to the neglected child, to her own failure as a mother, to the burnt cakes now smoking out of the oven. Written down, it sounds like a whine or a cry for help. It's both and neither, just read it as an act of colour, a fact of Leah's life.

(Now here comes the shocking truth. At this point, dear reader, you will understand that I had to choose between two of the other sisters as I had no intention of making this a foursome: far too many people in the one, single bed. Which should I choose? Each of them is equally nasty, selfish, self-seeking and prepared to do anything to get what she wants – even to poisoning other people, even to fighting over a bloke, vilifying her father and hating her sister. Mr.S's choice of names leaves me with a problem: Regan is the name of a past, rather dubious U.S. President and Gonneril sounds like one of the more unpleasant S.T.I's – I am thankful that, in my teaching career, I have never had to encounter a child with this particular malnomer (to coin a word). So it's not really an alternative, Bad Cop is to be named Regan.)

Regan, nasty lady – quite the opposite of Cordelia. What she really wants is to be the centre of attention, to have everyone so afraid of what she does or might do that they are manipulated by her. She wants to be rich, she wants to be famous, she wants to be hated, admired and loved. She wants, basically, for Leah not to give a shit about anyone or anything except herself. In a sense though, Regan is better at looking out for Leah than Cordelia , so she is not all bad.

This leaves the final, the simple answer to 'Me' – I am Lear. However, for the sake of my own fiction and also to avoid confusion *(Edward Lear, King Lear, don't leer...)* I shall spell the name LEAH. Leah links nicely with sadness and confusion. *(As well as taking in the troubled, mad king, we also have a clever little biblical reference to Leah the unloved, unwanted daughter foisted off on an unsuspecting chap.)* The 'Me' at the centre of this most unequal triangle, feels pulled about, angry, bouncy, sad, suicidal/full of life, confused, happy/happy, happy/peculiar, unique/a speck of dirt, loving/hating, humorous/humorless, eccentric/ professional, capable/incapable, humbuggy/credulous and afraid that she is in process of losing her mind and thus just plain fearful and, like poor old Lear, carried away by circumstances beyond her control.

(There are two small points to address before I begin this journey. Firstly, if I am Cordelia, Regan & Leah – who is writing this? Secondly, Mr S also included a most significant character - the Fool. With regard to the first point, I have no intention of going down that route as K.L. put it himself 'that way madness lies'. In the case of the second point, my dog most adequately fills the role of Fool, he is both ridiculous and a truth teller. We converse on many subjects, sometimes he acts the giddy goat: can dogs be giddy goats? I think so, and if you see him chasing his tail round in ever decreasing circles, you will agree with me. So let the description stand.)

The scene is therefore set. Let me introduce the actors:

Leah (is me)

Regan (is me Bad Cop)

Cordelia (is me Good Cop)

Fool (is Dog).

I hope that you are not brassed-off with all of this scene setting, an inventory is essential so that I do not 'get lost' even though my selves will. *(In any case, you could of course skip this prologue – take a break why don't you? Have a nice cup of coffee – actually I rather fancy one myself... But no, I'm 988 words into this tale and I have sworn on my mother's heart that I will not rest until I have written at least two thousand words today, so onward, upward).*

The Tale

Leah treads with bare feet across the deep pile, wool carpet. It's one hundred percent wool and backed with expensive canvas. If she digs in her toes she can feel the most pleasant sensation: a bit like squishing the soles of her feet into warm sand only not so gritty. She moves with alacrity to the music-making-thing... *(The name of it escapes her, once it would have been a wind-up-gramophone, then a record player, then a tape recorder, then... and on into infinity. In this ever improving-up-to-date-must-have-gadget era, she preferred to think of the thing generically.)* ... She wanted to hear music, the music maker made music and that was enough.

She placed the thingy, in the whatsit, pressed a couple of dooburies and waited. Chet Baker peeled gently into her ears, she seated herself on the dark pink wicker chair, dug her feet into the carpet and waited. There was Chet, in her head tempting her with the words, "Let's get lost..." He croons, with messages for Leah, personally. "Let's get lost...let's get crossed off everybody's list...let's get lost". The refrain is there, get lost, get lost...

'Oh how I wish, I could get lost.' Sitting there in the chair trying hard to breath deep, to be mindful, to let go of the washing machine of thoughts swashing around. She breathes and as she breathes, she pulls in more thoughts, they crash against the wall of her skull, chipping off pieces of bone, flying apart in her head, piercing her brain, piercing her mind. She cries out with the pain of it all...

Regan takes her hand, "Yes, Leah. Dear, dear Leah. Here I hold your hand in mine, let me lead to another place, a kinder place where you can be you. We'll be so happy together." ...and in the crashing, Regan's voice is strong and clear, she leads Leah out of the chair, away from the cosy carpet, down the stairs. Shoes on, sensible shoes, says Regan; because they have miles to go before Leah will be allowed to sleep and Regan *(though preferring the six-inch-sexy-stilettos)* wants to lead Leah away in a certain amount of comfort to a place where she will be able to have total control at which point, Regan will become Leah, Leah will cease to exist...

Leah laces the shoes obediently, she takes a rucksack from the cupboard, some fruit from the kitchen and a bottle of water. Her hand hovers over her mobile - phone. "Oh no," says Regan, softly, "We're really truly going to get lost, we do not want to be found by anyone". Leah yields, replacing the phone on the dining table, for good measure, she switches it off. "Well done!" says Regan. "You know this is what you really want. Come, put on a warm jumper, put on waterproofs – it's raining."

Without warning, the Fool enters centre stage, bounding down the stairs, tumbling over his own tail in his haste not to be left behind. The Fool's tail wags eagerly, he smiles his unselfish, doggy smile, "Here, you cannot go without your best friend, get my lead. Take me with you Leah." He circles her legs, sniffing with his two noses, brushing her with his coat like a cat. The Fool has no clear idea of his caninity, sometimes he thinks feline but mostly human. "Oh Fool!" sighs Leah, bending to stroke his rugged back. "Fool, I cannot leave without you: we shall get lost together."

Enter Cordelia, hand outstretched in a full and meaning-filled dramatic gesture. Regan cusses under her breath, the voice scratchy, irritant. "Sod off Cordelia, this is my scene." Cordelia offers her other hand to Regan, "Why so aggressive Regan? She belongs with me, you have no place in her life." *(At this point, another voice makes them aware of its presence, it floats down the stairs: "…get lost…they'll think us rather rude…crazy mood." Chet Baker, lost in his own drug-perplexed world, lost with his own personal good and bad cops, 'Let's get lost.')* Cordelia, raises her voice, gentle-toned but necessary to guide Leah back to the reality of the Fool. Regan's words are muffled but still an audible whisper, "Leave the mutt behind, he's a drag, a bore – a tie…" The word 'tie' fades to silence as it is spoken. Firmly, Cordelia takes Leah's arm, leads her into the kitchen, kindly pushes her into a dining chair and begins to stroke her temples.

"Listen," Cordelia says in quite, reasoned tones, "Listen, you don't really want to get lost. You have so much to give, so many people depend upon you, so much to do." The patter of rain splashes against the windows, the Fool whimpers, pawing the front door. Leah shakes Cordelia's hand away, rises and states aloud, "At any rate, the Fool needs a walk, rain or no rain. Here lad, here's your lead."

The trinity marches off through the rain, it is pouring down in uncontrolled lashes, driven horizontal by the wind. The Fool ignores the malevolence of the storm and presses forward into the oncoming wind, his fur blows backwards, his ears flatten against his skull. "I am Fool, he seems to say, "I am humour, I am the truth no one else dares speak." Leah removes her specs which are now so plastered in rain she can hardly see the way ahead: her waterproof gear runs with water, her eyelashes, nose, lips – whole face is soaked. She elbows Cordelia aside, shoves Regan away and starts to breath again.

"Fool," she says, "am I an egg with two crowns and nothing in the middle?" The Fool considers, "This is possible, I think but not probable." "Fool," she says, 'what am I then? Who am I that I should be baptised with this rain?" "The rain," says the Fool, "Is not a baptism, it's a washing away, a rinsing – no more that that. Come, let's run."

And they run and they run and they run through the pounding precipitation, through the stinging conversation with the foul weather. Leah laughs, the Fool laughs. They are laughing because they are foolish, this late-middle-aged woman and her hirsute dog. She thinks of her moustaches, which have to be kept under painful control, threaded once a fortnight – no escape, she doesn't want to be a mustachioed lady. Regan calls "Why not? Why do you have to deny the proofs of age? The crows-feet-scars earned in the battle of life? Come, Leah, let yourself go. Join a circus!" "Ah," replies Leah, "Now that would be a spark of inspiration because I could take the Fool with me." Regan considers: Leah needs to get away from it all to wander into the unknown, to truly get lost. If the Fool comes, then so-be-it, he can always be sold off, given away or... Regan mutters the word quietly to herself, 'destroyed...' Leah cannot hear the word, she is already charmed by the idea of the circus. "I would not like to be a bearded lady, this would not suit. For one thing, beards tickle, for another my hair is white but my moustaches are dark black and would not match. I shall buy a razor and take it with me." Leah begins to plan.

Money will be required for this venture – where can she get money from? "Obvious," says Regan, "'Cash machine – you've only just been paid." Leah considers this, but the limit is £300 a day, she would not get very far with that. "Then," logics Regan, "Go into the bank now and withdraw all your cash – the mortgage money doesn't come out 'til the first of the month and today is the 29th. Take the cash and go." Now, £2,000- give or take the odd hundred – is plenty of cash to get lost with initially. It would be enough to go a long way on foot, by bus and or rail towards anonymity. It doesn't have to be a circus, maybe London, Glasgow or some other big city where you could cease to exist, 'they' would never be able to find you: unless you decided you wanted to be found. You'd be able to sleep en route and the Fool could be fed and watered at intervals. Yes, this is the answer, take the money and run. Regan smiled to herself, 'That's right,' she soothed, find the real you..."

Ah, there was the problem. Regan had raised it and now it would not go away. Who is the real me? thought Leah. I've been searching for her for months and each time I think I've found her, she drifts away like Alice down the rabbit hole. Is the real me a thief? Thief because half the money in the account belongs to my 'Other Half', half the Fool belongs to my other 'half'. That's three halves, she thought, leaving me with my half which is in fact a quarter. So does that mean I'm only entitled to a quarter of myself? Tears seep from her eyes, mingling with the sea-salty rain. "Fool! Fool!" she cries out, "I want to be whole." The Fool looks up at her, bedraggled, run out, ready for home, he whimpers. "Home now?" questions Leah. "Home," says Fool. "Home," says Cordelia. "Fuck the lot of you!" shouts Regan, storming off to her lair.

Leah opens the front door; the warmth that meets her is soothing. "How ever could I think of leaving this comfort? How ever could I think this?" The Fool runs up and down the narrow hallway, shaking himself as he goes, rubbing his soaking coat on any piece of rug or carpet he can find. He snuffles and grumbles, "I'm wet, wet – do you hear?" he shakes and tosses his head about. *(Slips, trips and falls – take personal responsibility for your safety.)* He skids on a wet patch of tile and performs an unintended back flip. Slightly dazed by his own suppleness, he turns to Leah and barks, loudly, repeatedly, "Food for the fool," he says, "Food for the fool." Obedient to his command, Leah goes into the kitchen, fills his dish and lowers it to the floor. "Here Fool: take what is yours."

She strips off her wet clothing, retires to bed and despite the fact that it is the middle of the day, falls into a profound sleep. Regan, seated on the back of a large Indian elephant, enters her dreams, waving. "Imagine," she shouts, the red, purple and gold howdah rippling in the slight breeze. "Imagine, riding on the back of this elephant." Leah climbs up beside her, breathing in the raw smells of straw, canvas and dung. She calls to the Fool to come, but he is afraid and begins a series of terrified howling barks...

Leah wakes with a start, the Fool is on the bed, licking her ears. He wants her to wake up, to stop the stupid elephant-Regan-inspired dream. He wants her to be herself, just herself. Leah feels a heavy smack in her face. The Fool has arrived at the bedside with his ball-on-a-string. He issues a series of rapid, staccato barks, "play, play, Play, Play, PLAY!" Leah climbs out of the bed and, encouraged by Cordelia, plays. Regan, thwarted, storms but cannot be heard above the barking Fool. "Okay, okay," laughs Leah, "let's play."

Leah and the Fool sit at the top of the carpeted stairs, she takes the ball-on-a-string, commands "Sit...Wait...Paw." And, obedient, the Fool anticipates his reward. The ball wangs down the stairs, bounces off the magnolia wall, leaving a greasy mark: with urgent paws and eager legs, the Fool bounds after it, fully canine. He takes the ball in his mouth and shakes it from side to side, 'killing' his prey, then vaults back up the stairs taking them two at a time and the process is repeated. Leah and the Fool play on for some ten minutes, time passes quickly with shouts, barks and accidental nips. Each is so fully engaged with the other: to their chagrin, Cordelia and Regan cannot access Leah's head. That is, until the doorbell rings... *(The Fool, as always leaps about, yelps and growls and all of the other etceteras dogs do when provoked by doorbells. He knows the person (or persons) on the others side of the door is/are there exclusively to see him, he wants to welcome them in his shaggy little paws, he cannot wait to greet them.)* ...Leah opens the door, before her stands Mallory. Cordelia is immediately alert, Regan begins to scheme...

(A brief background will help here you to understand the significance of Mallory. One of Leah's weaknesses/strengths? is that according to the tenets of her faith, she must care, she must always be responsible and

caring. Mallory was one of her 'waifs & strays' as Leah's
'Other Half' described the woman.

So, a potted history of Mallory: She is in her late
twenties, homeless and an alcoholic: this despite having had
a highly successful career in hotel management. Against all
reason, Mallory stalked the Hotel manager, a married man
with a family. Now, this would not much matter in the
normal run of things, they would probably have had a fling,
a row and stopped before any damage was done. However,
the subject of Mallory's unrequited passions was a tea-total,
bible thumping, blonde bombshell, CHRISTIAN. His beliefs
were curbed during company time but he would exploit any
opportunity to evangelise: if he thought he'd got the pinch
on your soul, he'd never let go until he'd got your head
under the waters and claimed you for CHRIST. Mallory,
beguiled by his six-pack and sharp suits, failed completely to
understand this and started dressing for the kill. She donned
a slit skirt, low cut bustier, drenched herself in perfume and
shot off in panting pursuit. I do admit that he, being a man,
was seriously tempted; but the bustier and the fact that she
was off her face with vodka made him fall (metaphorically)
to his sinuous knees and pray for Mallory's deliverance from
the demon within. Sober, next day and the truth dawning,
Mallory packed her bags and traps and slunk off.)...Now
here was Mallory, again, quite off her face: disheveled and
smelly, weeping copiously; pleading for help, forgiveness,
money, a bed, food, a blanket, a bath, a shoulder – the list
is endless...

A speedy chat with Regan made Leah consider
offering Mallory a fiver and sending her away. To invite
Mallory in would mean endless maudlin hours of tears,
self-reproach, yelling, swearing, blaming succeeded by a
great shouting, not to say more extremely offensive
vocabulary – all from Mallory- finishing off with a
slammed front door. (*The last time this drama had*
unfolded, Mallory had managed to break the glass).
However, Cordelia took control and Leah succumbed to
the pathetic vision huddled on the doorstep. "I know,"

slurred Mallory, "I know I'm the last person you want to see or even to talk to but Leah, you're my only friend..."

Cordelia whispered reassuringly into Leah's mind: she needs help, she needs shelter, she needs food - a real friend that she can trust. Just think Leah, you could be her. Mucked up, messed up and washed out. It could be you Leah... Yes, thought Leah, it could be me and I'd be so glad of a friend, but the thing is that after last time had not gone down well with Leah's Other Half. He had expressed his opinion in no uncertain terms, peppered it with invective and made Leah promise that there would be NO NEXT TIME. But, Cordelia was concerned, you don't think he meant that? Admittedly he had every right to be angry but that was the heat of the moment...and the door was fixed...and at so little cost...well yes, that's partly because he did it himself but he likes doing odd jobs about the place...he will understand...you can't let your friend in need down.

By the time Leah had sifted through Cordelia's internal monologue, she'd ushered Mallory into the kitchen and was putting the kettle on. It was at this point Regan chipped in:" by gum don't you choose 'em and no mistake. HE won't be best pleased when he knows, have you really forgotten last time? What he said? You are an idiot. Do you not remember this morning? We could have been well away by now, lost in some cityscape, anonymous amongst a crowd of nobodies, you'd have been one of the nothing and no ones, you'd have been able to start again. You certainly wouldn't have been here to answer that doorbell. Fool!" And the Fool seemed to emphasise this point by leaping up at Mallory, licking her lachrymose cheeks. Which only made Mallory cry even more: "Oh you wonderful, wonderful doggy, you love me, you remember me, you forgive me." Which of course he did, and just to confirm the pact he did a tail chase round the room knocking into a plant pot, smashing it so that the soil scattered all across the Marley-tiled floor. Leah cried out in irritation. "Fool! Get out." And the Fool downed his tail, curled it quivering about his nether regions and slunk away.

As Leah made strong coffee and buttered toast for her distraught friend, an argument raged between Cordelia and Regan. Leah felt as though between them they were trying to batter her brains to mush, she wished they would go away, leave her be, leave her to find out who she really was. Mallory shook as she gulped the coffee down, Leah felt pity, Leah felt contempt. What did Mallory need she wondered. 'Like me', thought Leah, 'she needs to find herself, she needs to move away from the past, she needs to stop falling on her sword every day – how can she learn, how can I learn that once was enough? Mea Culpa, Mea Culpa, Mea Culpa – YES, it's true, now move on, start again. But how and who and what and why and where?' Leah was not at home in her own body, Mallory was not at home in her own body. What did this mean?

"It means," screamed Regan. "That it's about time you took control of your life, stop dithering, stop making sacrifices that no one wants and no one expects. Think of yourself." Cordelia responded, "Be true to yourself Leah, be true to your beliefs. Just because you've waded into a mind-mire now, it won't always be that way, you will find yourself, you will be at one with your own body, mind and spirit." Add to this conflagration, Mallory's whining wail and the Fool's incessant barking. Leah's head began to slide. She raised her hands as if to prevent it coming apart completely, she pressed her fingers against her temples, more pressure, she thought, more pressure, more pressure. She pushed and pushed until the joints of her fingers sizzled with pain. "SHUT UP!" Leah bellowed. "SHUT UP, SHUT UP, Shut up, shut up, shutup, shutup, shut..." *(Silence. The voices of Cordelia and Regan ceased completely; the Fool stopped mid-bark and looked at her enquiringly: he was mirrored by Mallory whose mouth remained open in an unseemly gape...)*

Before Leah could even consider her actions, she had kicked the Fool out of the back door and into the garden, her head stopped sliding and she began to focus on the pitiable wretch before her. She pointed a finger at Mallory "You,"she said in plain tones, "are real. Mallory, you stink. You need a bath – you know where the bathroom is, go take one." Mallory opened her mouth to speak but Leah cut across her, "Bath, now."

As Mallory disappeared up the stairs, Leah began to count the cost of living with her exploding mind, there just wasn't enough room in it to accommodate Cordelia and Regan: they must not be allowed to return. She let the Fool back into the now quiet kitchen, absent-mindedly fondling his ears: "Fool, we have to take charge. We cannot allow everyone else to run our lives. Not them, not you, not my Other Half. I am Leah, I am a mature woman. It's time for me to grow up." The Fool looked at her with knowing eyes, he'd heard this speech before. My name is Leah, he thought, And I am… but there was the conundrum, what was she? She didn't drink, so it wasn't the booze; she didn't take drugs, so her mind was not fuddled; she didn't smoke. In fact, thought the Fool, her life is defined by all of the things she doesn't do. He nipped the thumb of her right hand as a way of showing his agreement. They observed each other sorrowfully. Leah shut out the echoes of her good/bad cops: they whispered in the background like a badly tuned radio. Mallory returned, wrapped in a bath sheet, her hair glistened with water, her face, florid though it was, looked fresher. She was sober.

Leah made a pronouncement. "I have decided, Mallory, that you may take fresh clothing from my cupboard, and some money from my purse. I shall take you first to find a B&B and then to AA where you will begin to face up to yourself and start to put things right. I want you to understand Mallory, that after this, my door will be closed to you if you ever come to my home drunk again. I will not answer, I will not help you." And meekly, Mallory accepted.

Epilogue

What the future held for Mallory we may not know. All I can tell is that, thanks in part to Chet Baker, Cordelia and Regan 'got lost' . That night the Fool went for his evening walk with the Other Half: Leah went into the garden to dead head the roses. As she cut, she listened to the twilight calls of the birds, the voices of people also in their gardens, also dead heading roses and she was overcome by a new sense of self. She became aware of a new voice, "I am Pandora and this is my box..."

4. Micaela

I see her face in the firelight and remember my beloved friend, my adopted mother, Mercè. When I was a very small child, the fever came to our village and took away the wellspring of my being: I hardly knew them, they are just glimpses of memory which I sometimes snatch for in my waking moments. Madre Mercè found me, I was muddled up with the spring lambs in the meadow, singing softly to myself scenting the air which held all the promise of a country spring. I was unaware that the sleeping figures in the enclosure would never wake again.

Mercè swept me up that day, took me to her home: there was no one else. Indiscriminate, dispassionate nature had hewn a path through our lives. I remember the warm smell of maturing wine, intoxicating, fruity, heady as it wafted from the barrel in the cellar. So many scents mingled throughout the bodega, they soaked into my very soul. Hanging from the beams high up in the buhoudilla were great sides of cured meat, these gave off the musky smell of spices, the aromatic fragrance of herbs; this piquant bouquet a feast for the senses. As I grew, I played safely in the comfort of Mercè's arms, Mercè's store and most of all, in the warmth of Mercè's love. Madre Mercè, the only parent I have ever known.

José, her son, was five years older than me when Mercè brought me to her home wrapped in a sheep fleece, curled in her arms. Mercè had love enough for both of us we three were all in all to one another. He was a wild boy, self-willed, Mercè often chased him with her broom but he was so fast, she rarely caught him: even when she did, she never had the heart to carry out the threatened beating. Always, always we would fall together in gales of laughter at José's 'wickedness'. As the laughter subsided Mercè would say in breathless tones, "My son, you'll be the death of me." He would kiss her twenty times upon her gentle cheeks, pinch her and we would all laugh a little more.

José treated me like a plaything. He would carry me about on his back, hide me in the crates at the back of the shop and feed me stolen chunks of morcilla, jamón and chorizo. Mercè bartered goods in her shop; when slaughter time came round some portion of many a village pig was traded for spices, wine, herbs or dried wild mushrooms. Manifold parts of porcine anatomy were cured above in our small home; jars of oil and meat resided, sealed shut, upon the shelves in the cool back larder. We wanted for nothing. Mercè would have happily given José the treasured meat, but like so many other things, José preferred to steal it, 'Stolen fruits always taste so much better little Micaela' he would whisper as he fed me with his greasy fingers. In the seasons when fruit ripened he would fill my mouth with succulent sweet strawberries, downy honeyed apricots and lush flossy peaches – all stolen from the gardens and orchards of neighbours. Everyone knew José's ways, everyone forgave him time and time again – he was Mercè's son, he was a handsome charmer.

We grew together, small creatures, into maturity. José's body began to change, his voice to deepen, his beard to thicken. My breasts began to bud, my smell changed from girl to woman and I became aware of José's longing. Mercè was sensitive to the change in both of us: she was anxious for my innocence wanted me to be free, to be mature enough to make my own choices. "Micaela, take heed, you are yet young, there are others more handsome and less impetuous than our beloved José." I looked at Mercè in puzzlement when she said this, José was my brother, by affinity. "Madre Mercè, what can my brother do to me that would make you grieve?" Mercè merely smiled and with trembling lips, kissed my forehead.

Each autumn José and I went out to the forest to gather wild mushrooms. Mercè had taught us well, she knew which were safe, from an early age we had both imbibed this wisdom. We walked, talked and ran to the high forest trees. I was slender then and could press my body through the slightest gaps in the gnarled tree boles, José was more sturdily built and could not follow. In all our years of play, we had evolved a game of catch-as-catch-can, a kind of unhide-and seek. Early on this particular misty morning, we were taking turns to unhide – the rule was to leave some part of the clothing ill-concealed to give a clue to the seeker. My sky blue skirt was trimmed with bright lemon coloured ribbon it caught sparse rays of sunlight which pierced the canopy of lush green. The skirt was full, fluid: my body revelled in a longing I had never known before. When my turn came to unhide, I found a hollow trunk in an ancient Juniper. My skirt flared out around me, the lemon and the blue bringing light into the dark space within the heart of the tree.

José tramped noisily through the woods, loudly singing "Caaaaae - la! Micaaaaa -ela! Caaa-ela, Caela." He sought me out and laughing threw himself upon the ground beside me: impetuous José, laughing up into my face. I find it difficult to put into words the rush I felt at that moment, the change from fraternity to something else, an aching in my limbs, a longing in my mind? The word desire is too strong, my senses reeled, deep as oceans. They cascaded uncontrollably through my being: 'Michaela, take heed' Mercè's words whispered in my mind. Swiftly, in the fraction of a blink of an eye José caught my mood. He stopped laughing, in that second we seemed to stop breathing, the birds ceased their singing, the trees did not move: we were held in profound immotion, a still point in a turning world. José's face moved closer to mine. His sweet breath brushed my cheeks as he moved to deepen our embrace, his hand hovered closely over my breast but did not clasp it. The spell was broken abruptly by the thud of a falling branch. We moved away from one another and without speaking, continued our search for mushrooms.

That day, so long ago, so many worlds and actions lived through. It was not long after this that José joined the

Almanza Dragoons: I thought Mercè's heart would break when he paraded in front of her, the vibrant red and yellow of his uniform abrading our eyes like fine grit. "I'm off to seek and make our fortune and when I return…" He did not complete the sentence but bent his head, embracing both of us then turned and walked away.

For Mercè and I, life continued. We worked the bodega, cured our embutidos with salt and herbs then hung them from the attic beams. Each evening we sat before the fire and took our wine, damask hued, razor-edged upon the tongue. We were not bitter, we lived around the space that was José longing for his vibrancy, his vitality. Mercè and I comforted one another but our laughter was muted; our beloved clown was absent. Whispers of his life were brought to us by villagers who travelled to the market in Seville: José was having a high old time; José had spent his pay on liquor; José had lost a mint at pitch-and-toss; José sent his love, said that he would visit soon. For six months, no notes, no visits, no nothing except these whispers.

'Mi querida Madre, mi hermosa 'Caela,' the letter began, the first paragraph was a paean dedicated to us both, he told of his love, of the ways in which his wealth would change all our lives, he spoke of the fine dresses he would buy for us and the jewels that would adorn us. Mercè read this part of the letter with great humour, "Our impetuous boy, does not change!" we laughed loudly, no; José did not change. As she read the next part of the letter, Mercè's tone resounded with a disappointed acceptance, and a shoulder shrug. '…and so my dear mother, I don't like to ask – triumph and wealth are awaiting me, it's all so near but if you could spare me…' The castles our José built in the air, had Mercè refused him money at that point, might things have been different? I pause and think again of my beloved Mother Mercè's face. The firelight is flickering around me, shadows and shapes melt and blend upon the walls of our small home. The last time we all sat here, we laughed, loved and asked the burning coals to tell us our fates. Different? Ah, who can ever say?

That first time, I hitched a lift to Seville on Don Remendado's cart, the pungent, green aroma of earth and cabbages clung to my clothes as I walked to find José. We talked a little, I gave him his mother's letter and the money he so badly needed. As he tucked these into his tunic, José wept copiously, he choked out words of shame, words of apology: he had not meant things to be this way. I comforted him, told him how much we loved him, assured him that our strength was his to take. José dried his tears, embraced me, called me his own special niña: he built more cloud-castles, so real, I could see them as he spoke. I ran back to Mercè gleefully, telling José's news, saying how he looked and spilling out the many words of hope and love which had poured from his lips.

Over the next couple of years, the letters from our brave Corporal came sporadically, the content of promises and pleas for help unchanging. Many a time I rode to Seville on the cabbage cart, with his faithful mother's small savings. Always we embraced, always he cried: our belief in José became a hollow lip service. "If only," Mercè looked at me with pleading eyes, "if only this time, Michaela my treasure, you could persuade him to come home. He could go to the priest, then you would truly be my daughter, you would be my choice for my foolish son." Me? I shared the same dream, sighed with the same longing but though José always pledged his love to me he never mentioned wedlock. He was ever and always our impetuous, footloose, funny, naughty boy.

New whispers came to us from Seville of girls in the cigarette factory, of gypsies, dancing, singing, ever loosening morals. One name was oft-repeated 'Carmencita' woman of free spirit, a coquette who spoke shallow words of love for any man who took her fancy. Don Remendado's voice shook as he told me of Carmen "She's a witch, a devious enchantress – she will devour José!" he blushed and sweated, clearly Don Remendado had not been unaffected by her spell. "Little Michaela, Carmen is the very devil in women's clothing. You must get yourself to Seville... José must be saved..."

Now Don Remendado was an old man, not easily ruffled: in his long life he had seen much to make him weep. I took his warning seriously and left once more for Seville. The dragoons had become more pushy, the licentious atmosphere was infecting everyone. The girls from the cigarette factory were hot, the dragoons exploding with lust. As I walked into the square, I felt the threat of it all, I pulled my shawl tightly about me as though this alone would afford me protection. Don Remendado's son seemed to think I had arrived purely to fulfil his desires all of those men seemed to think they could pinch or stroke me without my consent. It was sickening. At last my darling José appeared, I took him to one side, told him of Mercè's love, of her forgiveness, of her blessing our union and her desperate need to have him home. We talked long into the evening, at times José seemed almost afraid, his 'castles' lacked conviction. I caught his fear and gained from him a promise that he would be with us soon.

News of José's desertion felled Mercè, her towering strength withered; she was left without the power of speech. The frozen muscles on one side of her face created a mocking half grin made all the more poignant by her ever falling tears. I told her that I would seek José and bring him to her: I left her in the care of neighbours. I walked through forests, climbed slopes, jagged my feet and clothes on rocks as I sought our José. Shots were fired, they scared me and I hid but after waiting some while in the shadows, I saw him.

José believed me when I told him that Mercè was dying, believed me when I said he must come home. He would, I think, have walked away with me then but for her taunting voice telling him to "run home to mummy." That voice and the mocking strut of that stupid torero burned in José's brain, preventing him from moving. I pleaded with him, tried to talk him home but even as I spoke, Carmen's string pulled ever tighter. Mercè was dying, she needed me even if her stupid son could not answer her call. Having lost all hope of success, I returned alone to Madre Mercè.

He did return, Don Remendado brought José home on the empty cabbage cart, his beautiful face covered with a scarlet shawl. By this time Mercè had fallen into her final sleep, death hovered closely by waiting to claim her. I was glad to have José home, sad that cold as he was, he would rest eternally with the mother who loved him unconditionally.

I am old myself now, I live alone but am never lonely as the bodega is always open to neighbours who come to buy or barter, to share some of my raw wine. We mull over the latest village gossip, laugh or shake our heads knowingly over the antics of the young. Don Remendado is long gone but his grandson is always ready to help me shift things for old times sake.

I breathe in the musty smells of drying meat and fermenting wine. I stir the flames, I see their faces, a burning splinter spits onto the rag rug before the hearth, I use the tongs to snuff it out and as the ember dies I send blessings to my two dear ones. I wish I'd never heard the name of Carmen...

5. Making Jelly Without A Mould

Imagine you want to make jelly. That sweet semi-transparent, semi-opaque, semi-liquid substance; those sticky-break apart, squares which used to come wrapped in brightly-coloured-waxed-paper stamped with the name Rowntrees. That transcendent-party-ambrosia-striped-rainbow-flamed-rabbit-shaped-sandcastle-shaped-dream-shaped-food made perfect with pink blancmange and sometimes (oh sometimes but rarely) made sublime with a slice of Walls vanilla ice-cream. (I'm digressing from actually making the jelly, but stay with me, there is a point to all of this – from now on, 'digressions' will be marked with ** fore and aft so that, if they annoy you, reader, you can simply skip them and get to the heart of things). (p.s. if you really want to get to the heart of this (well I was going to call it a story but that doesn't fit) ah, yes, the heart of this revelation without having to wade through the substance then (dear, dear reader) stay with the title, which says it all...)

Imagine a time when the concept of that great white box of a freezer, maybe in your kitchen, garage, utility room, whathaveyou, did not exist. Now I know this, for those born a little after my time, this will be an impossibility but, imagine. Long before my time when the rich ruled the world (as they still do today) before a freezer or electricity or anything so unimaginably amazing as that had been invented (I still don't know why electricity doesn't leak out of the walls and form a pool on the floor, please don't try to explain, you will fail as others have failed before).

Where was I? Oh yes, the truly olden days. The **Poshgits** had icehouses built in their gardens and the icehouses had thick, thick walls and were filled with blocks of ice which had been towed from the icy-regions-of-the-world (or something like that) and put in the icehouse so that the **Poshgits** could eat icecreamicecubesicesculptures &oystersetc. In my childhood, I'm not sure what the **Poshgits** had – perhaps an entireicecreamvantothemeselves? Well, we didn't have an icehouse, we were proletariat thus in the scheme of things of no great importance, in fact not important at all. Anyway, we had a **FRIDGE** a greatcreamycoloured caverngood forbaconmilkcheeseandstuff – but ice-cream would just melt. So the point is that **IF** you were having a children's party and **IF** you wanted to serve Wallsicecreamsoldinabrickwrapped inwaxed cardboardmostlyvanillabutsometimes(ohjoy)sometimesn eapolitanpinkbrownwhitestriped, **IF** as, I say, you wanted to serve said ice-cream it had to be pre-arranged. In our village that meant a discussion with the postmistressvillageshopowner to make sure the ice-cream would be there at a time given to collect it, then an arrangement with my older brother to ride to the shop on his redRaleighbicyclewithSturmeyArcherGears to pick up the ice-cream. It had to be the exact moment as the jelly was about to be served but before the happybirthdaytoyoucake was broughtin flamingcandlesandall.**

Making jelly may seem a simple task, which in many ways it is but in some ways it isn't. I've defined clearly what **I mean** by jelly but of course, you the reader may have different ideas. You may perhaps be a **VEGAN** in which case the thought of pigs will float into your mind and the thought of traditional jelly will float right out. For those of you who do not know, carnivore jelly is made from gelatine, gelatine is made from the bits of pigs which polite society considers to be inedible(tailsnosesearsteeth trottersskinetcbutnosqueak). First all of these bits are put into a bucket of acid (or the industrial equivalent) and soaked to leach out the collagen. Then, when all of the gunky stuff has been leached out, it's strained and boiled – a wonderful piggy soup...

As well as used in making jelly to eat, gelatine/collagen a bovine or porcine by-product is used to **fillyourfacein** in when you've gone a bit wrinkly round the edges, though for the sake of veracity I must add that there aresyntheticalternativesavailable.

...then they do something else with the pig-soup to make it fitforhumanconsumption and then it gets used in many different ways, which I shall pass over, the most interesting of which to me is jelly. But, because I want to be fair to the Vegan readers amongst you, you can also get Vegan Jelly Crystals where the gelling agent is made from carrageenan and locust bean gum. Interestingly carrageenan is made from carrageen which is an edible red seaweed: and locust bean gum comes from locust pods (not locust insects) and were, for those of you who have met with him in the past, the very locustsJohntheBaptist ateinhiswildernessyears ***(and very nutritious they are too).***

So to, coin a phrase never used by the eponymouscoook
mrsbeeton 'first catch your jelly'. With immense apologies to the hairy-piggy-huggers amongst you I have to say I go for the genuine gelatine variety every time. Shaking a packet of jelly crystals into a jug does not have the same appeal as
tearingablockofRowntreesjellyapartwithmyownbarehand s. I wonder if this is my primitive hunter/gatherer instinct emerging from the annals of my human history? What fun, the need for the chase (visit to the supermarket) the hunting down of my prey
(choosingthepacketfromtheshelf) and the kill
tearingablockofRowntreesjellyapartwithmyownbarehand s. There it lies before me on the kitchen counter awaiting **THE BOILING.**

Now here we hit on a snag. I cannot sufficiently emphasise to you the necessity to readtheinstructions. If you are my era or older and have
NOTMADEJELLYSINCEYOUWERE

ACHILD you will discover that the method has changed. My mum taught me to break the jelly into bits, putitinapanwith
halfapintofcoldwater and heat over a gas flame until the jelly pieces were dissolved. Then you topped the water up to a full pint, poured the whole lot into a glass dish and left it on the backdoorstepbythecoalhousedoor to congeal
*(or if you prefer 'set', 'congeal' conjuring up images of dried blood.)*Nowadays, as opposed to Oldendays, you measure out your 500ml of cold water, break the jollyoldjelly into a **MICROWAVEPROOF CONTAINER**, pour 100ml of the water onto the jelly, melt it in the microwave: stir, add the remains of the water: stir again, pour the jelly into a
mouldicecrubetraydishdishesorwhat
haveyou and place the aforementioned in the fridge to set.

Retrospective: That amazing moment of anticipation at a friend's party when the sandwiches (joyofjoymurmitesandwichspread&spreadycheeseencasedin slicedwhitebread) had been eaten and in prospect was the jellywithallitsetceteras. I always felt a sort of greedy fullness, having eaten so much, I always feared I would be unable to fit in the jelbrosia without being violently sick. Actually I do remember now that it was not uncommon for me to throw up after a child's party – the cause? Too much excitement, lack of minute personal hygiene on my/my host's part, orange juice the colour of a radioactive isotope or just pure unbridled greed? I know that I was relieved when the alltoosickysweetbirthdaycakewithicing jamandrealbuttercream was given to us by the front door on departure, wrapped in a sweaty bit of paper napkin, placed in already gluey fingers for us totakehomeandsharewithoursiblings. This is a marvelous retrospectiveprospectiveandIamenjoying themeandering.

So there we have our carnivourous jelly, liquid feast – but of course if you choose to consume it now it will simply make you vomit and that would not do. You must

CHOOSE theshapethatwillsuityourwildestdesires. Now there is a wide range of ways to set a jelly. Far, far wider than when I was a child. I think that it was poured into a cracked white bowl and doled out that way, posher homes would have a proper glass jelly dish and really posh homes would serve it in frilly, gaily patterned waxed paper dishes. (Interesting the degree to which waxed paper enters into this narrative, was there more or less of it when I was a child?). Nowadays choosing the shape of jelly is no laughing matter, given the extensive social vocabulary of a modern toddler you could, by choosing the wrong shape, brand or colour of jelly, cause that child expensive traumas which will affect him/her for the rest of his life and cause therapists of many different shapes, sizes, flavours and colours to become exceptionally wealthy. But of course in the last clause I was actually referring to the offspring of the Poshgits rather than the ones belong to the plain old proletariat , in other words the majority. There are many ways to mould a jelly, these may come in silicon, glass or plastic, I have chosen just a few of them to give you an idea: halloweenmaskbirthdaycake jellybabypenisbreasts(withnipples)flowersboats&bears – even, thank the lord, rabbit shapes.

Did I really write penis and breast shaped jelly moulds?... I've just checked back on the website and sure enough, there they are large as life and twice as nasty. If ever I went to a party with a jelly penis and breasts (nipples or no nipples) I think I would go extremely red and walk out. Just had a really happy thought though, I never go to or get invited to 'that' sort of party, not my cup of tea at all

Now to my way of thinking one of the very, very best party jellies of all times was a rainbow striped one in an imposingglassdishofancientorigin the mother of the birthday girl/boy must have spent days composing this work of art. It consisted of layers of different coloured jelly in richardofyourgavebattleinvain order. Now this was the crowning moment of all jellies because SHE intermingled water jelly with jelly made from whisked up evaporated milk. If you have never eatenaprincelyjellyofthisvariety it behoves me to describe it to you, mouthful by mouthful right now. But I can't a. it would shatter my illusions and b. it's quite beyond my creative powers – this jelly was beyond description thus I am obliged to leave it up to you to use your own powers of invention. (I also advise you never to attempt this venusdemiloofpuddings as the actuality will never match your fancy).

So there you are, in your kitchen with your jelly and your chosen mould. You pour it in, wait a few hoursheypresto there'syour*****(fillintheblankforyourself)shape. You turn it out for the delight of your amazed audience and within seconds, the whole thing is a memory (until the next time).

IMUSTJUST *share another reminiscence with you of one of my* **FINESTCREATIONS *it was intendedironicallyofcourse designed to amuse some of the most refined of pulates. I was in possession, at the time, of a glass rabbit jelly mould* **ANDA RECIPE** *for carrot&tomato pate. I made the pate, poured into the glass mould and served my rabbit on a bed of real green lettuce. At the front end he was nibbling a fewjuicymrmcgregortype carrots; at the back end I placed a smallpileofblackolives My rabbit was the centre piece of my* **Poshgits** *style dinner party and a* **HUGESUCCESS** *sotresamusent.***

Given this stylish, intricate (pleasdon'tsayboring) build up, you are probably on the edge your seat wondering how the title links up to the purpose of my *story/reflection/recipe/ sermon/address (deleteasapplicable) and the actual answer is this: to make a jelly without some form of mould, how ever simple would be foolish. You'd pour it out into infinity and it would seep downthesideofthecookerintothecracksinthework topunderthefridge&ontothefloor. The resultant sticky mess would attract wasps, bees, flies, dogs (some cats) and would be impossible to ever clear up without dismantlingyourentire kitchenwhichyouwouldnotliketodo. So the point has to be, prepare an appropriate mould before you begin.

But why am I telling you this? What is the hidden meaning? It's like this. For the past fewdaysmonthsweeksyears my own personal sense of reality has been on the blink. It got to a point where I felt so battered about the psych and so beleaguered in the soma that I ceased to function. I sat in an armchair and stopped.
    So, I'm using the jelly as an
ANALOGYFABLEPARABLE
EXAMPLE to help you understand where iam/amnot. Some days are good days where everything is in order, the jelly is in the mould and though it might be a little sticky round the edges, is definitely recognizable as jelly in a seemly sort of shape. But then there are other days when the jellymissesthemould reality oozes into inaccessible places and my poor cerebrum rocks and rolls about like fallen mercury. Reality takes on the shape of unreality, I think I have donesomethingspokentosomeone and find when the blinking stops that this is not the case. On the other hand, as the jelly drips freely and moulds itself to the shapes it touches, I find that actualrealencoutnerswithpeopleplacesandthings which have taken place have been wiped from my memory or seem so dream-like in quality that I question their authenticity. I have, of late, taken to double checking with people justtomakesure although it has to be said that this does not reassure me…
    I realise that the 'problem' relates to my current lack of a mould. Never before has my time been so free. My'fitnotes'are 'unfitnotes'i'mnotcompetenttodomyjob and as time passes I doubt that my competency will ever return. With my head I can understand and analyse what is/has happened; with my body I can recognise its

strengths and its limitation BUT my mould has been broken.
MakingjellywithoutamouldisIMPOSSIBLE

6. The Lingering Memory of Purple

I awake with a smile and the lingering memory of purple sweetens the day. The light outside is growing as early day rises into the consciousness of the outside world. The traffic, quieter in the nighttime, now begins to bruise my hearing in this place of almost never silence. Unreality and reality collide in a mess of sounds, they all but wipe my waking mood.

My first port of call is to the loo for a long and satisfying wee – something about the first wee of the day, hot, rushing, splashing into the toilet pan with a new day glee. I wash my hands, the soap bubbling between the webs of each of my fingers, then rinse them in freezing cold water. As I dry them I sniff their cleanness, I love the smell of new washed hands, the scent of soap and the coldness of fingers after water. In the kitchen I begin the ritual.

Large brown Denby jug, poised to make the perfect cup of coffee. The kettle boils, I warm the pot, I place the plastic filter on the top of the jug and inside fold and place the filter paper. One, two, three, four scoops of coffee. The dusty fragrance teases my senses. The kettle, now off the boil, is lifted and the first splash of water lands on the waiting grounds, the full and bitter smell of roasted beans seeps into the air. I wait for the coffee to drip through. Now, you may watch this performance and wonder why I don't get one of those smart espresso machines, or at the very least an electric filter jug or one of those burbling pots that swills and snuffles before boiling over on the hob, or perhaps one of those press and go things. I have tried them all, but none offers the slow, meditative satisfaction of making my own coffee, drip by glorious drip and awaiting the result.

We hurry into days, take them headlong, busy, Busy, BUSY. We shout at ourselves to go faster, get appliances for ourselves that do things faster, we drink the coffee faster and get out of the door FASTER. Time is flying by, got to get ahead days, days which leave you in a wilderness of panic wondering where the time went, how you can make it up by say, missing sleep or waking earlier. We live in this ever pressured bubble of a world, who knows where the time goes?

I have tried fast moving coffee, fast moving life, it makes me thin in the mind, squashed into a flat state so that I can post myself through the tiny cracks in time, the milliseconds and moments to be made the very most of. I realise now that I was spread so thin I was in effect, transparent. So, I jettisoned coffee makers of all kinds, bought the Brown Denby Jug for a fiver in a junk shop and slowed the pace. The coffee, cradled in my hands in a Wedgewood coffee cup designed by Susie Cooper – '70s Diabalo pattern, the geometric loops of tan and black interweave across the thin bone china surface, I smell before I drink. The coffee lingers in my nose as I take my first sip, gentle on the tongue initially then sharp, black, uncompromising flavours awake all of my senses: make me feel that I am alive.

By the way, I do not possess a set of Wedgwood coffee cups, just the one cup without a saucer. I purchased it for three pounds, so adding things up and taking the jug, the filter, the filter papers, the actual coffee, the water and the electricity used to boil the kettle – I ponder for a moment the cost of this cup of coffee now warming my belly. Of course, I have forgotten the manufacturers, the Fair Trade farmers, the hands that plucked, the machines that ground. I make a cursory nod to all of these aspects, say a thank you but still cannot calculate the cost of this cup of coffee. To sling it, unthinking down my throat and to race work-ward without another thought about the coffee, except perhaps, how to deal with my coffee breath *(chew minted gum, graze mouthly like some cow in some field)*, to sling the coffee and race off in this way would be a sacrilegious act, an insult to all of the energy used in giving me this single pot. I rest awhile, put my back against the cushions of my ancient, bumbling, sagging sofa and relish the coffee as my mind tunes into the beginning of this new day.

The purple memory returns, I catch the thought, the dream, the memory of what? How to explain?

You were born so suddenly. Are you sure you are pregnant, the midwife asked, or have you just swallowed a pickled onion? I laughed, you were such a neat package inside me, kicking at my belly with your long legs, curling and floating inside me. Was I pregnant? Yes, your life, within my life for 37 weeks. I remained slender throughout, even so, as was the custom, covering my bump with discreet, loose fitting maternity dresses. I envy the young mothers now who, without any kind of shame or doubt parade their beautiful bellies as they bloom into fullness. Tight tops, displaying the fabrication of a human being. I touched the belly which carried my grandchildren and felt them kick: an action never even considered when you were growing inside me.

Once, just once you kicked your father in bed, I was asked to move away, he was one of the type – we mothers *(then)* accepted that fathers had nothing to do *(beyond the one act)* with maternity, childbirth and child rearing: I was not offended, just sad that he, true to his generation, felt unable to join with you as you grew. As you ripened, my uterus grew with you, a flexible ball of amniotic fluid to cushion you from the world. I forget exactly when, maybe I was about 34 weeks forward, yes, probably about that, I was gifted with this amazing dream.

I rest the Susie Cooper Cup upon my now rounded, empty abdomen: empty even of the womb that sustained you and later your brother. I think of you both, now men and recall that though many years, months, days, minutes and seconds have passed, I will always be the nest in which you were nurtured. You and he were both part of me, just as I was part of my mother: like so many Babushka Dolls opening up into the infinity that is past, present and future. No one can take this truth away from me.

That dream. The power of pondering should never be underestimated, so much can be caught in the ponderer's net. So much that is of comfort when the mainstream, the BUSY, Busy, busy mainstream of life seems to wash away all feelings of self-worth, of self itself. This dream then.

You humped your back up in my rounded belly, you rolled and reached and as you did so your hand, somehow, some miraculous how, grasped mine. We held hands through the wall of my stomach, through the boundaries of my womb: you, my first-born made this special contact with me the life giver. Just that. I awoke from that dream, knowing that something extraordinary had happened. I felt like silk, like sunshine, like the joy of all the days. The dream stayed, stays with me. When I think of it I want to dance. Circular movements, touching the memory, holding your foetal hand, so long grown up and grown away from me. I move slowly, thinking of you, thinking of that empty space where you used to be. I know that you are still mine even as you belong to your self. This brings me bliss but also sadness.

Susie Cooper, now empty, rests on the elm coffee table. I look at the rings and the patterned scars caused at some stage in the tree's life by a fungus. They dart about the buttery surface of the wood like little shooting stars. I run my hand across them and wonder about the tree that gave life to this table. An indiscriminate showering of seeds, scattered across some autumn sky. The earth was mother to this tree, nurtured it through the seasons until the small seed geminated and broke her surface.

Have you swallowed a pickled onion? the midwife asked. I chuckle at the memory, proud of my skinny body with its swelling breasts. 'They' have decided that it's time for you to emerge from the safety of my womb into the world. 3 weeks too soon, but even so all is prepared for your arrival at home: the soft, sweet smelling toweling nappies, the baby oils, powders and creams with that distinctive pinky baby smell, the Moses Basket – all lined with blankets, all ready for you, my first born: ah, you think I should write 'son' in this place, we did not know then, could not know the gender of our labouring until the very moment. I was so excited, I wanted to rush forward into this new aspect of our relationship, to greet you, to know you.

Five hours later, after a lot of groaning and moaning *(mine)*, and encouragement and bossing *(theirs)* you slipped from between my thighs, so suddenly. So suddenly, it did not seem possible. I held you, briefly... this baby needs to rest, they said. I lay, ecstatic, the hard part was over, we could begin. Little did I know: at that moment I just thought of you. Your face filled my mind: the nurse told me that you were awake to life from the first second, your eyes looked around, searched for light. My nosy baby.

The ritual of clearing away must begin. I have delayed the day for a while, I have wrapped myself in memories of you but now, the day must begin, I must engage. But what about the purple memory? I smile to myself once more as I wash the empty brown jug and rinse the coffee cup twisting my fingers round the lip to make sure that none of my germs stay in place. Strange the need for this action, I am the only one who drinks from this cup: Susie Cooper is mine in this respect. And yet, she must be scrupulously cleaned, then placed upon the hook ready for the start of tomorrow. This time spent washing out my coffee cup gives more time for reflection, more time to recall that particular purple moment.

After you were born, after you became yourself, a unique person: I felt bereaved. Strange that, how can birth be a bereavement, but it was so. I lay in the warm hospital bed, the stiff, starchy sheets covering my body. Instinctively I listened for your kicks, I felt little ghost kicks, traces of you inside me: but you were gone. I felt afraid. Whilst you were inside me, I had control, I knew that I could care for you, wholly and solely: the ghost kicks seemed to me a mockery, you were resting in the nursery, out of my sight, out of my hearing; I was also resting, but afraid. Were you real? Had I imagined you? I asked a nurse, she said that you were well, that you must rest, that I must rest. I rested, uneasy empty arms with ghostly kicks to remind me what was lost.

Your father came later in the day baffled by your so sudden birth: *I was on a building site, I was wearing borrowed wellies because of the mud, I didn't know.* We neither of us knew then: knowing, true knowing comes with time, familiarity, triumphs and errors. You were resting.

I hardly remember the lazy days in hospital where I learned to feed and bath you: they kept us in for some immeasurable time in those days, controlling visitors, giving you your baby at feed time and getting you to rest. I hardly know how young women cope these days, hot bedding as they do. Babies come without user manuals. Common as the earth's dirt, you and they rely on instinct, the helpful *(sometimes most unhelpful)* advice of others who have trodden this path. Those days I spent in hospital, waiting my release, waiting the day when I could fully claim you as my own. It's only now that I appreciate them, glad that I was not required to drop and go.
We took you home one sunny spring morning in February. You were wrapped in a white blanket wore a babygrow, white with stripes on the feet and sleeves. 3 weeks early, so tender, so precious, so unsayable – no words for this, just overpowering, un-namable emotions that swill about me. We took you home.

The coffee cup is now resting upon its hook, the brown jug is poised for action on its heat proof mat, the filter, filter papers and coffee tin are packed away. The day must begin: but wait, let me complete the purple memory.

We took you home, your father drove with care and I cradled you in my arms – no car seats then. Sleeping, you were laid in your Moses basket in the warm front bedroom created for your use. A wooden rocking chair sat still in one corner, your white cot gleamed at me and your baby-changing mat – I think it was spotty – but maybe not – your changing mat was placed on top of the red, folding, Formica table. All was ready: we, you and I were on the road. You were peaceful: and I? I desired the freshness of the outside air; I felt the need to feel the weak warmth of the spring sun. I left you, knowing you were safe, I left you in your space and walked out of the brown back door into the garden. I observed the scene. The apple trees were already coming into blossom so pink they were, pink as sugar, pink as snow in the moonlight, they radiated light. The grass was green and short, it was still in winter mode but spiked in patches seeking the light above its blades were crocuses. One special crocus seemed to speak to me its effulgent purpleness drawing my eye, drawing me into that moment. That moment last fractions of seconds, even now I'm glad I caught it.

I felt at one.

7. The Wardrobe

Please don't misunderstand me, I'm not proud but I do have my pride. My gentleman was a refined man, his taste was understated, his appearance immaculate: I was glad to serve him until the day he died.

I watched as he was laid out: that of course was after the family left, they'd been with him right up to the last dreadful gasp. His final word, 'Mother', breathed so quietly, so hushed: they were devastated. But she, brave woman that she was, insisted on doing the laying out with the help of his Valet. My gentleman had a Valet, no expense spared in this household though he was a single man all his life. They prepared him for glory in total silence, in a beautiful harmony. She tied his chin so lovingly, her hands moved gently over his face and head, you'd have thought she was trying not wake him. His Valet stripped off his clothes and folded them so neatly. Once his limbs had straightened, they washed him with scented soap and clear water. Each limb, raised, washed and lowered – all so very correct and dignified: just like my gentleman. Finally that white linen gown, scented with lavender. It had been washed in blue, dried in the sun, starched, each fold and seam pressed flat. I looked at him as he lay there his arms crossed over his chest: I was the only one who stayed with him every second until they carried him out, it was right that it was I who kept constant vigil.

Once they had carried him out that was the last I saw of him, they wouldn't have thought...it would not have been considered...possible even but at least I knew about the funeral from my gentleman's servants. They came in to clear and clean the chamber, they were not responsible, not in any way for what happened to me...later: but I anticipate, I want to reflect now on his funeral procession. Black ostrich plumes for the horse which pulled a black carriage with his lovely polished elm coffin, brass handles and all. The coachman wore black, the mourners followed behind – all in black. The family had done it right they said, the mourners had their black gloves and all the beautiful white cotton handkerchiefs, bordered in black. Black, black all of it black I like to think of him, my gentleman laid to rest, properly, decently buried.

It was only after they'd cleared his room, cleaned and waxed polished every bit of wood 'til it was bursting with effulgence that I understood things would never be the same: if I could have seen the future, I'd have begged to be eaten by the worm and consumed by flame there and then. You see, I was his armoire... 'Amour' I hear you say in your ignorance believing this is some sordid little love affair of which I am about to 'kiss and tell' – the popular phrase I believe for such revelations. I was privy to all of my gentleman's innermost secrets, they will go with me to the grave, should I ever be allowed the singularly human privilege of death. The word is ARMOIRE or in rather prosaic English if you prefer, his wardrobe. And not just any old wardrobe, flamed mahogany of the most expensive kind ever grown. I have majestic doors which reach almost to ceiling height, graduated drawers with perfect dovetailed joints and four deep linen trays. My gentleman's suits were all of the highest quality - Barathea wool, silk neck-ties, silk linings of the deepest burgundy and cloth covered buttons, handmade silk waistcoats in a rainbow of colours and designs, shirts of pure white cotton and always, always the scent of lavender. The warmth of the fabrics, the hot smell of a newly laundered and pressed shirt: these things were meat and drink to me. When my gentleman stood dressed, oh so immaculately by his valet, he was the equal of kings. I am not ashamed to own that I loved him.

After the chamber was cleared of his possessions, some rather crude and ungainly men arrived equipped with notebooks and pencils. Their voices were far coarser than any of the maidservants I ever encountered and the language they used... I would never demean myself by repeating it. I particularly disliked the short, rotund one who tipped his hat while eyeing up the furniture and licked the end of his pencil before scribbling figures onto his tablette. Ugh! They ran their greasy fingers all over my woodwork, scratched at my inlays – they even slammed my doors. To add insult to injury, when talking to my late gentleman's mother they laughed in her face and called me 'unfashionable', not the kind of thing anyone would buy in this day and age. She wept bitterly, she at least knew our value – may I say beyond pearls? I suppose not because they sold a three string of pearls at auction for fifteen times the price I achieved. I speak figuratively and assert without a blush, that my value is and always will be, beyond that of pearls.

This time I abbreviate. Down the years I was auctioned, sold on, stored, carried on carts and finally dumped in a room – which I now know to be 'some horrid little sixties bedsit', I still shudder to recall the smell from the gas ring coupled with the stink of ammonia emanating from poorly washed baby's nappies hanging over a cracked basin. No one polished me then, no one cherished me. It was so much to be borne, too, too much and yet, un-waxed, unpolished, despised in so many ways I could do nothing else. Imagine when, after all the screaming, blood, sweat and palaver, they laid a scrawny baby in one of my dovetailed drawers. They had lined it with some horrid inky-smelling newspaper, the 'thing' was swaddled in its father's shirt and squalled and screamed without ceasing... Then they were gone.

Years went by, mice nested on my shelves and gnawed a little at my frame, a leak in the ceiling allowed water from a blocked sink in the room above to drip, stinking, onto my beading. The bedsit couple had painted my doors in what they called psychedelic colours, my flamed mahogany could no longer be seen. The glass in the windows of the dwelling first cracked and then broke as vandals threw empty bottles or stones through them for a drunken laugh. Occasionally a shivering tramp would seek refuge from the cold in the room where I stood but mostly

I was alone with the mice and the decaying floorboards; my weight an increasing threat as the years went by.

Then suddenly it all changed. A man in a sharp suit brought another equally sharply dressed woman to 'look the place over'. These people were quite unlike the horrid bailiffs who'd shipped me out of my gentleman's home though their accents were not what I would call 'refined', they still exuded a certain something. I heard words like, 'merchant's house,' faded grandeur', 'Georgian' all accompanied by gasps of joy, chuckles of exuberant excitement. I watched and listened as they crawled over the entire house 'wowing' all that they saw, measuring, laughing loudly, calling each other to 'come here and look, oh look, look, look'. After that, a string of people marched through the place with their dirty workman's boots and hard hats. Tape measures and pick axes, cement shovels and brick trowels. Some had flasks and sandwiches, some ate pies but to a man or woman, they were a dirty dishevelled lot with not the slightest hint of amour-propre. I tell you, in all of my many years – first in the forests of the West Indies, then in a cabinet makers workshop, to my gentleman's dressing room – even with all of the tramps, tarts and other filth that have paraded before me – never in all my considerable number of years have I witnessed such scenes of depravity. It is and remains unspeakable.

However, rescue came in the form of the following conversation, and I quote it verbatim: (Long haired individual, scruffy appearance, his (or possibly her) face has been stapled in several places and a snake tattoo runs across the neck, disappearing down the front of his chemise which is emblazoned with the word 'Firetrap' and has some kind of geometric pencil sketch scribbled all over the front – he's not even wearing a neck cloth!) The accent seems to be quite cultured: "Bugger me Jus – come and have a dekko at this cupboard thing: must have been the mutt's nuts in its day. Reckon it could be worth a bomb".

I was somewhat shocked at the invitation to 'Jus' to engage in sodomy – but that's modern people for you, no sense of decorum – but when this did not happen I began to realise that I was the 'cupboard thing' to which he was referring; as for 'mutt's nuts' and 'bomb' the less said the better. He pressed a few keys on his 'mobile' and within the hour a man from Flockson's Auction House appeared. Now this comforted me, the name 'Flockson' was one I'd heard on the lips of my gentleman more than once, when he was dressing, he would talk to his Valet about the fine art works he had obtained through their good offices – could this be one of the heirs of Flockson?

More tape measures, more notes, more phone calls and conversations. It seemed that at last my worth had been recognised despite my degraded circumstances. In short, I was rescued, restored and sold at auction. My 'unusually fine flamed mahogany doors' were what raised my value – I will not lower myself to name the sum but I will give a hint that four figures were involved and those four figures represented a price well beyond that accrued for those three string pearls. Who, I mused, could have the taste and refinement to wish to possess an armoire of my quality? Would it be, I wondered, a new gentleman with his own Valet?

I confess that the shock of my new circumstances left me reeling with shame and indignation. I was re-homed in a 'lady's' boudoir I say 'lady' but the woman to whom I refer was called 'Shiraz' and spoke with the most appalling twang. The boudoir was decorated in various shades of sugar pink and her bed was draped round with a silk canopy, the Louis Quinze meublle de chevet either side seemed to me to shiver with embarrassment – I know I did – every time I observed the full sized daguerreotype of a nude displayed on one of the walls. It left NOTHING to the imagination.

Shiraz filled my trays with flimsy silken things – bustier, plunge, push up and balconette brassieres, g-string, v-string and rhinestone t-back thongs. She possessed whips, paddles, ticklers and dildos; corsets, handcuffs, a purple vibrator and innumerable quantities of male prophylactics in a rainbow array of colours and textures. My trays, MY TRAYS! My dovetailed drawers were defiled with her strangely styled clothing. I would have preferred the squalling baby wrapped in newspaper to this. Then there were 'les amis' – three of whom she seemed to be especially fond judging by the whispering and whatnot that went on. I will not lower myself to describe how Shiraz carried on with her BFF, as she called them, I shudder to recall it all. Screams of 'OMG!' reverberated round the room. Squawks about 'LBDs', 'HoboBags', 'Spritzing', 'Faves', 'Raves' and 'Flirt Alerts' bounced around me until I could stand it no longer.

And now she is dead: you want details? Why is Shiraz's body lying crumpled on the floor? How you ask? ...drugs? ...alcohol?...a furious lover? No. It was a conspiracy between myself and a former colleague. Colleague, yes that's right, you have not misheard me. You want to know more? I suppose it can't hurt – even if you do repeat it they'll have you locked up because, as everyone knows, an amoire of my quality keeps secrets.

It was like this.

This evening, Chardoenay comes rushing in "OMG you'll never BELIEEEEEVEEE what I just found!" She squeals and dances round the room like something gone mad. Then Shiraz, Merlot and Wallflower all begin to scream, prance shriek and laugh – the cacophony was intolerable. I peered out to see what they were crowing about this time – perhaps a backless, frontless pair of knickers without seams or gusset? And then I saw it...

I remember the first time he wore it home that full-length frock coat. It was made from highest quality tweed and had a brown velvet collar and cuffs, the buttons were covered in the same velvet. Three buttons were fitted to the front, three to the sleeves and two to the rear. It was lined in a brown polished cotton and had two flap pockets at the hip. I sighed out loud it really was my gentleman's coat. One of them – Merlot I think or perhaps Wallflower shrieked "OMG what the f*** was that?" Shiraz laughed and said, "It's that friggin' wardrobe, it creaks and frankly freaks me out." Chardoenay said, "Well get rid then – your place your space." "I probably will, after the photoshoot next week but it's like iconic – y'know, kinda like glam, timeless – a sort of LBD of the furniture world." ...and then they all went out of the room in a huddle, wine glasses in hand, becoming increasingly inebriated by the minute. We could hear their muffled voices as they paraded through the house: always such a relief to get the place to ourselves.

My gentleman's frock coat lay moaning on the bed, I called out gently at first and then a little louder, "Is that you?" I said and gave a tiny cough. "I say Frock Coat my dear chap, is it really you?" And it was! Had either of us been able to weep, we would have flung ourselves, each into the other's bosom and wept copious, joyful tears. But we were limited by our respective states of being. Frock Coat's tale was not quite as harrowing as my own – he had been wrapped in tissue, placed in a trunk with some other garments, peppered with mothballs and forgotten. The trunk had been opened about a month previous and Frock Coat had been purchased as a gift for Shiraz. What on earth, I thought gloomily, could this fiend in feminine shape want with a coat of such quality? Something, Frock Coat told me to do with the photo-shoot. When I explained to Frock Coat what this would mean, he broke down completely. One of the meublle de chevet tried to murmur words of comfort in lilting French but poor Frock Coat was quite beside himself. It was then that between us we hatched a plot. Each of us felt for our circumstances, the come down from quality was too great, Shiraz had to go.

Frock Coat quivered somewhat at the part he had to play in her disposal but we cheered him on with words of encouragement: for the honour of us all, he had to do it, he was the only one...

Shiraz returned later this evening: her crass,

simpleminded companions had departed, she was quite alone and pretty far-gone in her cups. However, when she saw Frock Coat, she could not resist giving his velvet collar a tender stroke. At that moment, I almost felt sorry for what we had conspired to do, I could see that she had some perception of his quality: it was not enough. I watched as Frock Coat lay trembling beneath her touch, would he have courage? Her next action left me in no doubt.

Shiraz was wearing one of her less outrageous costumes – a maize coloured, cut-away, silk blouse: the gold embellished neckline (if you could call it that) reached to her waist, falling open to reveal the outline of two very unnatural looking breasts. Her linen, oxblood skirt covered her upper thighs – just – and was patterned with tiny diamond shapes. As I watched, Shiraz reached down to remove the powder blue shoes she was wearing; the six-inch stiletto heels ground scratch marks into the ancient oaken floor. She slowly stroked her ankles as one by one she loosed the straps: she threw each shoe, with a deliberate aim at the silken hangings around the bed and as they fell, the heels tore the fabric into fine shreds. Laughing like the drunken hag she was she began to perform a lewd dance before the full length, freestanding mirror in the corner of the room. With each movement she removed another garment, until she stood before the mirror completely naked. I held my breath as she reached out to pick up Frock Coat to involve him in this degrading spectacle. It was this, more than any other action on Shiraz's part that strengthened his resolve.

One by one she fumbled those slender bronzed arms into his sleeves, the cuffs draped over her hands hiding them from view. She hitched them up, pulling the tweed fabric across her breasts, even with the buttons done up, the coat hung loosely off her shoulders. Shiraz's hair, long, curled; dyed an impossibly shade of orange, draped seductively over the velvet collar. She raised her arms to pull the coat closer to her body: it was then that

Frock Coat acted. As she luxuriated in the warmth of his wool, she raised her hands to caress her throat with the velvet cuffs. A sharp sudden crack and it was over: Shiraz's neck was broken...

Now the room is quiet and empty again: we, the furniture of quality are waiting, wondering what will happen next. Each of us has survived for at the very least the past 150 years: though our styles may go in and out of fashion, we will always be valued because we cannot be replaced. I hope to serve a decent gentleman again, I trust he will have a valet.

8. Everything

The phone had rung half an hour ago, Lorentia had boomed out, "Lily? Good, now listen my girl, the casting committee has given a great deal of thought to their decision and I sincerely hope you appreciate this in the light of... Well, we don't need to mention that do we?..." and Lorentia, in her bounding, bountiful way had told Lily that THE PART was now hers for the taking.

As she put the receiver down, Lily began to reflect on this signal from the village that she was now accepted. "Whoever would have thought it?" she whispered to her cat, Joffrey, as he purred luxuriously beneath her stroking fingers. "Oh Joffrey, I've always hoped for this – can you believe they have given it to me? To ME?" The cat rolled over onto his tummy, Lily continued the silky massage of his to treacle-toffee spotted coat.

He gave a deep, contented, rumbling purr before putting a paw up to her cheek and yawning "Are you sure they have offered it to you?" Joffrey's sagacious voice cut across her thoughts. Joffrey was a six-year-old Bengal cat and Lily's most trusted companion.

"Joffrey, how can you doubt it? Lorentia was quite, quite clear, they wanted me. The committee have considered all of their options and plumped for me – despite... despite... well despite everything." The word 'everything' was breathed out sotto voce as if saying even that much aloud would dispel her dream.

Joffrey 'harrumphed' loudly and leapt from Lily's lap onto the floor where he began his habitual yoga exercises: from the deepest recesses of his magnificent fur coat he commenced a cross examination "Lily, why do you believe you have to appease these people?"

Lily looked back at Joffrey, startled, "Joffrey, why do you of all cats need to ask -getting THE part seals all."

"And yet Lorentia chose to remind you of your diminished, disreputable status?" Joffrey prompted, whilst meticulously licking his paw and cleaning out his handsome left ear.

"To be reminded is no bad thing Joffrey, it will help me keep on the straight and narrow in the future."

Joffrey paused, paw in mid-air, his pale, citron green eyes fixed on Lily's blue-grey ones, "The cost of Harvest Down society comes at a high premium: is it worth it?" The paw came down gently on his rump, adopting a soothing circular motion.

"You know Joffrey, I wish I could do yoga like you..." She looked admiringly at his lithe shape.

"That would be quite impossible ..." he paused and gave a polite purr, "...humans are so awkwardly formed – I am continually amazed that you can support that great lumbering body on just the two legs. However," Joffrey said sternly, " We are not discussing my superior abilities. I posed a question, you, Lily, have evaded giving an answer."

Lily looked at Joffrey thoughtfully: was it all worth it? "Joffrey, I'm going to make some coffee." He responded with an irritated mew. "No, I'm not avoiding answering... I just need to..." she broke off as he wound his sensuous body around her bare ankles. "Oh Joffrey, you are such a sweetie." She scratched his neck, "Is there something you would like?"

Joffrey stretched out appreciatively, he loved having his neck scratched for him: it was never quite the same when he did it himself. He had grown almost fond of this wayward human, "I'll have a little of the roast chicken – breast please, no bones – and if you wouldn't mind turning the tap on for me..."

"Of course." Lily leaned across and turned the cold tap far enough to create a gentle dribble. In a single bound, Joffrey was on the stainless steel sink lapping the water with evident delight. She watched for a while as the kettle boiled then turned to the fridge: Joffrey loved many different types of food but chicken remained his all time favourite. The coffee percolated into the glass flask: not her preferred brand but she'd make do.

They sat together in peaceable silence: she sipped Joffrey ate meditatively, savouring each bite. The hush was broken by the sound of a voice calling "Hello?" from the hallway. Joffrey raised his head and sighed, "Petula needs to learn courtesy." He sniffed and returned to his chicken.

Petula strode confidently into Lily's living room, she had assumed the role of confidante, nothing could shake her of the conviction that she was Lily's best friend. Joffrey watched as Petula seated herself on the couch: he neither approved nor trusted her. "Beware, Lily..." he murmured as he settled by the fire.

"Coffee – great, I obviously came at just the right moment." Petula smiled, took a mug and poured herself a cup of the steaming brew. "Mmmm – is this that Christmas blend I bought you? I think I can detect the scent of spices."

"Yes, the very last few scoops. I have enjoyed it," smiled Lily. Joffrey looked at her: the liar, he thought, it had been the only packet of coffee in the cupboard used now because Lily had forgotten to buy a fresh supply of Arabica. He would never fathom the complexities of the human mind. The fire was well stoked up, it suited his mood, as he reclined on the rug, ready to hear the conversation.

"I've heard," Petula's eyes were bright with gossip, "that you, my dear Lily have got THE part. So thrilling." Lily lowered her eyes, good girl, thought Joffrey, try to keep her at arms length. "Yes, I am pleased." Lily spoke low.

Petula looked slightly startled at this reception, she was hoping for more. "I should think you are more than pleased after..."

"After what?" Lily stared directly into Petula's eyes.

Petula shifted uneasily in her seat, "Well... you know... everything." She spoke tentatively, confidentially.

'Everything', such a convenient portmanteau word in which to pack past misdemeanors. No need to refer to the definite article, no need to explain: those in the know, knew, those out of the know could wonder. (Or, if fully accepted into the Harvest Down fraternity, Lily's story would be repeated through pursed lips in hushed whispers and horrified nods.)

Lily remained silent, Joffrey stretched his approval and moved nearer to the fire. "I mean," said Petula, now fumbling for the words which would ensure she avoided saying 'IT'. "... I mean that people are glad, glad to know that you..." she hesitated.

"That I...?" enquired Lily and waited

"Well, you know, the things that...those things that, happened, err, what you..." Petula broke off. She wondered why she needed to prompt Lily who had once been glad to tell all.

"Petula, I'm not entirely sure I know what you mean but I'll tell you this. I am presently considering whether to accept the part." Lily looked at her frankly and awaited the next incursion of her private life."

Petula sat back contemplating Lily's statement 'considering'? How cool could a person be? Six months ago Lily had been glad to fling herself into Petula's arms, seeking comfort from her alone. No one else had been prepared to pick her up. Petula treasured the ever-embellished memory of that evening, when Lily had wept openly and told ALL. She took up another stance, "I know, dear, it must be so painful for you to recall: and of course to know that everyone is aware. But there is no need, the past should stay exactly where it is, in the past."

Joffrey detected the odour of singed fur and decided this was the moment to sit upon Lily's lap. So infrequently do cats express their opinions out loud, he was considering which few words to choose: Joffrey wanted no misunderstanding.

Lily smoothed out his sleek coat. She was glad she had been chosen by a Bengal. They had had to come to certain understanding initially about things like the electricity bill and the concept of the water meter. He was fully conversant with the Internet but Lily had needed to explain the eccentricities of her printer to him. She refrained from comment when the morning paper had been shredded, in places where, whilst he read the financial pages, Joffrey's claws had caught. These small inconveniences failed to mar their friendship. Joffrey was always pleased to accept Lily's apologies when she got things wrong.

The silence became too much for Petula, she had wanted more, a great deal more. She had wanted to deliver a picture of Lily's abject gratitude to the fraternity, she had wanted to see Lorentia's face when she realized that Petula had beaten her to the post, had witnessed – person to person – the depths of Lily's appreciation. She wanted to give a blow-by-blow account of Lily's humble amazement at Harvest Down's munificent gesture. But Lily was giving her nothing – except the coffee which was, revolting. Petula put down her mug, "Dear girl I can't stay long..." she paused hoping that Lily would assure her that her company was desired. Lily did not speak. "I'm just so pleased for you," she placed a hand over Lily's, surely this was the cue for a disclosure? As she did so, Joffrey's claws cut unexpectedly into her skin. He looked up, Petula was too startled to react: she stared back at Joffrey. He spoke.

"Two things, Petula. Firstly, ask yourself if 'everything' you know about Lily is so? Really, really so. And secondly..." he rose, removed his claws from her hand, arched his back and sighed, "We would be grateful if you could remember that doorbells are for ringing, coffee is by invitation and, having each other, neither of us require a friend of the bosom." With that, Joffrey slipped from Lily's lap and sashayed from the room.

"I think that is Everything" smiled Lily. "I'm sure you will let Lorentia know that you have seen me." Petula opened her mouth to speak but no sound was forthcoming, Lily filled the gap, "And before you leave, I would be grateful if you would place your mug in the dishwasher, please ensure my door is firmly closed behind you." Joffrey yawned: 'time' he thought 'for another session of yoga'.

9. Life

Reflections on Picasso's painting 'La Vie' (Blue Period 1903)

As I walk into this picture I notice the tense faces of all around me. The room is an unsympathetic, Spartan sort of place. The bed is covered by unmade, rough blankets, there are no sheets, no pillowcases on the striped, stained pillows. The smell is sour, unwashed bodies, unwashed clothing, unswept floor – who would wish to more than touch the surface of this dark hovel?

She stands tall, clutching the small bundle in her arms, her face defiant. I cannot see her hands: the cloak - or is it a blanket? – is draped about her covering her from shoulder to ankle so completely: there is no hint that she is a woman, no woman's shape, fall or curve it is her face that tells me what she is. Angular, the nose long sharp, hair is pulled back tightly from the forehead, no nonsense. But the eyes? They tell another story.

I see the faint brush of age upon her neck, senescence shadows her. Her feet are harrowed; these feet have walked the hardest paths: hauling up, prevailing against many weathered days.

The smell from this picture is: Decay? Despair? Disgust? Discovery? Perhaps all of these things, perhaps none. As I enter this room, it smells of dirt, un-emptied chamber pots, a sleaziness that I would rather avoid and yet it draws me. The more I look, the more I seek to stay.

The woman in dark blue carries a bland and sleeping baby in her arms. This baby's face is hard to read: it's maybe three months old, it's sleeping. By contrast with the woman, the baby's face is young old, old young, wise, unknowing. This is something which might be said of all babies. Are we born all-knowing only to shed this wisdom as we learn to speak, learn to lie, learn to conceal who we really are? Or are we merely tabula rasa, something to be written on by life? This baby could be either: I have encountered babies, who could, should they choose to speak, tell things about me that I do not know myself. My granddaughter is one such. Her eyes penetrate, they tell me: 'fear me, if I could speak, if I could but speak...' She makes me shiver, in spite of my delight in her laughter. She is chubby, cuddlesome, she smells of soap.

This baby is hard to read, hued in shades of blue – his hair is a grey blue fuzz, the same shade is used for the features of his face; his wrap is ice-blue contrasting directly with the woman's black-blue cloak; the folds emphasised with a gentler pigeon-blue. Is this the tale of a confrontation?

Is this a story of mortality? Shadowy figures hide beneath and behind the main characters. Beneath the bed, almost blue-greyed out of sight crouches a figure – male or female? I am unsure. I imagine it to be a woman, her knees drawn up to her chin as if in pain, as if in the pain of childbirth. Hard labour, the greater memory of which is held in the woman's arms. Is this the essence of what I see? The woman in the foreground is she the mother of the man/boy whose naked lover clings to his shoulders?

The severity in the woman's face has nothing to do with hate or hurt or even anger: she has lost. This man/boy's body was once her sole property: she owned him complete. He grew within her womb for 40 weeks, she his whole world and entire life support system until he was expelled from the Eden of her uterus. I think of my sons: I feel a pang of pain that they are no longer mine. I once knew every part of their bodies. My vagina made a tunnel for them to seek the world. So great an intimacy cannot last. This is right, the child is father of the man, the man moves away from his mother, his body becomes a secret: he chooses with whom it will be shared.

These days, when I reach up to enfold them, they are giants of men, strong towers. There was a transition when I knew that I no longer 'owned them', they owned themselves. To chastise them I had to chase them but they were faster than me, I needed a stool to stand on to reach more than the backs of their legs. On one occasion my first-born coming into the kitchen to demand food. I was cooking the supper, he was told to wait. He went to the larder door, I stood in front of it to prevent his entry, he grinned, picked me up and put me to one side. The power shifted. Is this what this woman understands?

The woman stands with the memory of her infant son in her arms, the memory of his birth in her mind and sees the future, the future which does not include her. Had these two lovers, so slender, so perfect in their bodies, had they run away, were they hiding in some squalid squat? Wherever they are, she, the mother has found them.

The lovers have heavy eyes, the man/boy's are particularly dark, her eyes are downcast, his confrontational. I explore the picture and see that only one hand is revealed, the rest are concealed behind backs, behind cloaks, wrapped away, unseen. The man/boy's hand is raised from his waist, a finger pointing at the woman. 'Step away,' he seems to say, 'Step away, you can have no part in this.' I share the knowledge of loss with the woman. I watch my sons now with a mixture of pride and aching, aching jealousy. A son is your son 'til he takes him a wife...' So the old saying goes, it's a bland, black truth. If you love your children without conditions, truly, truly unconditionally, then they must fly from you. This joy is pain, it comes within the cup of motherhood: you hand them on to other people, to another person.

I sometimes wonder when I became a separate person, a woman/child in my own right. I dip into my memory and find a freeze-framed picture of a child of five. She has been asked to run to the post office, the money is held tightly in her right hand, she keeps repeating to herself, 'Two tup'ney stamps, two tup'ney stamps.' for this is her mission and she must not forget. In her desire for speed, to show that she is a grown up girl, she runs, trips on a pothole, grazing her knees on the gravelly surface. She is hurt, she opens her mouth to cry out for help and the cry dies upon her lips: there is no one. She is quite alone. This fact impresses itself upon the child, she rises, brushes off her knees and continues with her mission, shaken but now sure of herself. There is no one.

In the picture the woman/child clings, there is a wonderful symmetry about her closeness to the man/boy. Her peaking breast shadows his chest, her belly rests against his manhood: this neatly disguised in a pair of loose fitting pants. Her left leg is almost entwined with his. (*One hand, one heart - marriage was ordained for a remedy against sin, and to avoid fornication; that such persons as have not the gift of continency might marry, and keep themselves undefiled.*)

Fornication – now there's a word to conjure with. Are these two fornicators? If so, they are living in sin and perhaps the woman – if indeed she is the mother – is right to come and claim her own. We do not speak of fornication in the modern age, it has no place in our language. Fornicator suggest licentiousness, lewd behaviour. Couples who love, the straight, the gay: the couples who truly love create love, generate it by the bucket load, so how can they be living in sin? Woman, move away, let your son go, he has made his choice: learn to love her.

Lastly in the background, two shadowy figures embrace, arms entwined about their naked bodies, knees drawn up close, one of the pair – I cannot decide which is male – maybe they both are, maybe both female? – one of the pair, has their head tucked tightly beneath the chin of the other. What is Picasso trying to tell me? He left no clues, painted this picture and moved on to the next and the next and the next – the ever-rolling process of creation. Is this the key? With its many subtle shades of blue, the birth at the beginning, the man/boy/woman/girl, the embrace and back again to the birth.

When I first entered this picture I was overcome by the trenchant smells, what do I sense now, as I move away? I got used to the smell the more I looked: the more I listened to these characters who have been playing out their oil-petrified existence for the past hundred years, the more I sensed. It is not a foul smelling place, just the sweet and agéd scent of ambergris, musky strong smells of real human beings who once stood before an artist who stood before a canvas and who painted what he saw. I have made this picture mine: the child does not belong to the woman, the picture does not belong to the artist. We step away from that which we create.

10. The Farewell

The house had a history when we bought it: there was no doubt about that. Just as there was no doubt about the need for extensive renovation and updating. It charmed us both, suited the possibilities we dreamed of. Now, don't get me wrong, this was no stately home, far from it. It was a 3-bed semi built in 1933, it had a long thin garden, drab clad walls and metal windows. It also had that certain something.

When we viewed it the place had been empty since the owner, an elderly man, had died nine months previously. A china rabbit peered out of the landing window, in the hall, beneath the stairs there were stacks and stacks of tinned food, out of date, dented, rusting. The kitchen floor was covered in filthy old Marley Tiles, pale blue, the walls of the rooms were either painted in mouldy green or covered in peeling, gaudy '60s wallpaper. There were fitted carpets throughout - they stank of rot. The garden was tangled with weed, through which the original flowerbeds could be glimpsed: three apple trees promised a good harvest. There was a shed and a garage at the top of the garden: you could not get inside piled 'junk' of many different kinds barred the way. Yet this house, despite all appearances, did not feel neglected but truly alive. 'Welcome', it seemed to breath. 'I choose you.'

The decision to buy is of course, only the first step in acquiring ownership of a home, there are many trips, slips and falls to be overcome before you finally get the keys, so it was a few months between the decision and its realisation.

It's funny isn't it that when you have longed for something and it finally comes true, you suddenly feel daunted? There seemed such a lot to do, would we ever, ever complete the work? The first thing to be done was to get the decaying carpets to the tip. Amidst clouds of dust and a volley of rather choice swear words, they were wrested from the grip of the floors where, over the years, they had rotted and bonded: even so, they left little remembrances in the way of torn carpet strands, these would need to be scraped clean before further decisions could be made.

In removing the carpets we found 'treasure' in the form of a wood block floor not, as you might imagine, in the first flush of youth but a wood-block floor in herring bone pattern and very well worth restoring. This had been laid in the living room, the hall and the tiny downstairs room we named 'the snug'. It was this floor that began to give us evidence of the house's history.

We had learned much about its poignant past in the process of buying. This house and the one next door had been owned by members of the same family since 1933, the old man who died was the last of them and we were the first unrelated people to live in there. The Whitman family had lived in this house, and their married son in the neighbouring one. The house that we had bought had been bombed in 1943 resulting in the deaths of Mr & Mrs Whitman senior and their young daughter – the daughter had been found lying in the garden. Once the war was over rebuilding began using the scarce materials available: hence the luxury of the wood block floor, which was in fact, off-cuts of wood. Mr & Mrs Whitman, junior, had moved into the newly rebuilt house and sold on the house next door. Years passed, Mr and Mrs Whitman raised their daughters who married and moved away. Mr Whitman remained there until his death about ten months before we bought the house. What of Mrs Whitman though? I discovered that the poor soul was living in a nursing home, senile, crippled by a stroke, unable to get out of bed but none the less alive.

As time went by, our restoration works continued, before and after our daytime jobs, we hammered, chiselled, scraped and smashed. From time to time Ronnie, my partner, would go up into the garage and poke about, he found many treasures including a brass jug with the date 1918 hammered into it, an old shell case, soldered together to make a jug: 'Trench Art'. We still have the jug all these years and many moves later. The china rabbit remained on the landing windowsill overlooking the road at the castle lands opposite. As I write this I glance at Rabbit who has also moved with us. She stands upon a new sill and now has a view over the harbour.

The bathroom suite was real nasty '60s stuff – aqua blue with aqua blue veined tiles. We decided that for the sake of economy that we could clean up the old tiles and replace the suite with a plain white one. I was tasked with cleaning up the tiles. I began, they were a bit loose in places, as I worked it became clear that they were loose in many places. They fell, without warning and with an almighty crash smashed off the wall like a pack of stacked dominoes and dropped into the bath, the sink, onto the floor littering the bathroom with hundreds of shards. Having been dubious about the vile veined tiles anyway I was rather glad that expediency would, in this case, overrule economy.

All the time I worked on that house, as we used every available hour to turn it into a home, I felt that I was being watched. Approvingly I knew, there was no hint of menace about this presence.

In the attic, Ronnie rolled out great blankets of loft insulation; men with noisy drills made holes in the external walls and filled the cavities with bobbly beads of foam. It was as if the whole house had been clothed in a gigantic tea-cosy. On the day the newly installed central heating was turned on for the first time, the house gave a great purr of contentment.

Even so there was still so much to be done, the bathroom remained a mess, all three bedrooms needed the wallpaper stripping off. We hired a steam stripper for just 24 hours, ever trying to economise where we could, and I got the job of stripping off the walls within the allocated time slot. I went to it with a will, even with the steam stripper, it was no easy task. In addition to the steaming, a lot of hand scraping was required to clean stuff off the walls.

The clock ticked round towards midnight, the final room was still to do, walls and ceiling: my arms and shoulders ached from reaching up, the steamer seemed to become increasingly heavy. I shifted it and the ladder into the last room, brushing my forehead as I did so, 'Phew,' I said aloud, 'I could really do with some help on this last one.' I put the steamer down and trucked off for a wee. When I returned to the room two sheets of ceiling paper had peeled off and were hanging down. Was this the result of all the steam blowing about the place or had Mr Whitman answered my cry for help?

As the months went by, the house started to shape up to our expectations, there were the usual disputes about colours, wallpapers and functions but on the whole, it was very agreeable, this home of ours was increasingly becoming what we wanted it to be. Four months in we were had almost reached the curtain making stage and had acquired two rumbustious kittens who batted about the house, up and down the stairs then fell asleep where they stood.

It was November, the nights were cold, the 'Snug' made a very cosy retreat. On this particular night as rain lashed against the widows, it was dozily pleasant to have the coal fire glowing out its warmth from the hearth. I had earned time off from house 'stuff' that night and was curled up with the kittens, reading a book. As I dozed over the fire I became aware that they were observing something I could not see but could feel. A benign joy radiated into the room, moved to the living room, the kitchen, the bedrooms – every corner of the house: the kittens followed with eyes and paws.

The following day I heard that Mrs Whitman had died on the previous evening. Had Mr Whitman waited in the house for her to join him? I like to think so. I like to think he waited for her so that that they could make a sort of farewell tour of their old home before entrusting its future to us.

11. The Sound of her own Voice

Tremendous excitement bubbled in Liza's heart as she clambered up the old, slightly dodgy looking staircase: this is the day. This is the day when she could revel in the sound of her own voice; revel in the life she would give to the words from her own heart. Local Radio had appealed for 'ordinary' folk to write and record their Thoughts For The Day; on hearing this, Liza had rushed to her keyboard and looked frantically for the link. All the time, praying, please choose me, choose my voice.

Life, lived in a haphazard shower of incomplete circles, had never given Liza the opportunity to explore jobs in radio. When her children were young, she had been a stay at home mum, radio had been her lifeline to the wider world. Radio had been a friend; breaking up her days with visits to other countries via 'From Our Own Correspondent', gentle laughter with the characters in 'After Henry', confidential cuppas with 'Woman's Hour *(often her awareness was raised to an uncomfortable level when she heard discussions about FGM, Erin Pizzey and her women's refuges)* but always, she felt the comfortable presence of women like Sue McGregor. For as long as she could remember, radio had formed a background to her life, the pictures were always clearer, the ideas more challenging.

As Liza climbed the stairs to the recording studio, she tried to recall when radio had first been a conscious part of her life. It had begun, more years ago than she cared to remember with Listen With Mother. The voice of Daphne Oxenford – 'Are you sitting comfortably?...' a liquid chocolate voice that flowed its way around her child mind - so familiar; and after the story, the gentle notes of the Berceuse from Faure's Dolly Sweet building and fading gradually making her feel sleepy and warm. The picture she had in her own head of Miss Oxenford, unique to herself, no other human being could be in possession of

Liza's personal image of that voice. Every day, not long after dinner, Liza would snuggle down in one of the tatty old, mouldy-green armchairs and be transported. Funny how she could not now recall a single story, yet Daphne Oxenford's voice could be conjured up by an ear memory in an instant.

The steps were steep, the studio' was situated up several floors of the Old Post Office. A cleaner's bucket stood sloppily on one of the landings, the sour smell of a dirty floor cloth filled Liza's nose; there was, she accepted, little of romance about the reality of a radio studio. She paused a moment, to catch her breath and to massage the twinge of a stitch in her side. This pain reminded her of the sad day when she was obliged to bid farewell to Listen With Mother.

It was after her first momentous morning at infants' school: a mix of faces appeared in Liza's mind's-eye. The day had been a dark, damp September one without any of the redeeming features of early autumn. The large room had been crowded with children of all shapes, sizes and smells. One boy, who wept in copious quantities, had a green candle-wick of snot permanently dripping onto his upper lip. A girl with what looked like spun gold for hair, shimmered as the 'new children' were asked to line up (there always seemed to be lining up at school, infinite, deplorable, apparently pointless): as the girl with the spun gold hair stood in front of her in the line, Liza could not resist putting her lips to the hair and giving it an experimental lick. Hardly a whisper of a touch, hardly a breath and the taste of Sylverkrin Shampoo reached her senses at the same time as the girl, definitely confident for her age, asked Liza to stop it. That morning had consisted of a lot of waiting, the gentle voice of the aged teacher, more pointless lining up, sitting down, folding arms and listening. At the end of it, Liza was rather glad to go home for her dinner. It had been interesting but now she'd done it, well she was glad that was over and it would be a relief to engage again with her friends on the radio. When the truth dawned, she felt heart-broken but was quite unable to express this as silent tears seeped from beneath her eyelids. Her stoical mother returned her to afternoon school. 'You'll settle, in time,' mum had said. Up to a point, Liza had 'settled' but remained baffled about 'the point of it all' for the duration of her school days.

She chuckled to herself as she recommenced her ascension of the stairs. In pre-teenage years there had been Pirate Radio London *(only to be listened to under the bed clothes using a transistor radio borrowed from her older brother)* crackling with subversion. Radio London seemed to be the peak of perfection, Sandy Shaw, the Beatles, the Stones, Dusty Springfield *(her dad called her Rusty Springboard)* and other, other voices lost in the ether of time. One summer holiday her brother had purloined their father's reel-to-reel and they had recorded their own version of pirate radio. She chose to be called Angela, the project was doomed to failure because he was a dedicated pro and she wanted to meet up with her friends. For a second, she thought an old lady thought, was the music 'better' in those days? Maybe, but more likely, it belonged to the youngsters just as music, unintelligible to Liza in the present day, belonged to the youth.

Liza paused at the top step, three floors up and a smart little landing with a glass door labelled Local Radio. On closer observation, the doorframe had seen better days and the carpet where she rested her feet was fraying but, what the hell? She pushed the door open, her legs and stomach fizzing with excitement. A tall man, skinny, with a kindly face but terse manner stood before her: he was dressed in a windproof thermal jacket which was plastered in dry mud. He looked down at the mud: "I were commentating a match Sat'dy ha'n't 'ad chance to clean up. Name's Brendan McCullogh."

Liza smiled vacantly at him and shook his hand, a picture flashed up in her mind of Brendan, microphone in hand commentating a rugby scrum from the inside – perhaps they had used him as the ball? "Liza McArthur..."

he did not respond, 'Thought For the Day?' had she made a mistake? Brendan's face lit up with a smile. "Oh aye, I know, I was asked to come and set you up."

'Mind you, you'll 'ave to wait 'til after traffic,' She looked at him blankly, 'Goes out live'. Liza smiled again, not understanding. Admittedly it was coming up to rush hour, maybe another person would arrive to operate the equipment? Brendan took Liza's coat and indicated that she should wait until required: the chair was a battered office type with a wobbly wheel. To maintain her dignity, Liza had to jam her feet firmly on the floor or risk spinning about. Brendan took himself into a glass 'broom cupboard'. A red light went on. Brendan plugged his head into some massive cushioned earphones. Liza watched the dumb show at the same time as tuning into the live stream broadcast she could hear over the office Tannoy: the traffic report.

Through the thick glass, Liza could see a bank of dials and switches, levers to press up and down, a whole world of mystery to her: but the smell of it, the sharp electrical smells of the amplifiers, the odour of ingrained fag-ash, spilled coffee and electric wires filled her senses with a nostalgic longing. Her dad had been an engineer, had been fascinated with the technology of his day – how much more so would he want to be a part of the internet age? He was long dead: would you be proud dad? thought Liza as she enjoyed the moment. She'd never been able to tell with her father, sometimes he made her feel like the most beautiful child in the world, at others? Not so much a failure as less than adequate, a sort of could do better daughter. This day though, she was sure he would be pleased, would give her guarded praise, ideas about how to polish up her work.

The red light went out and Brendan emerged from the studio. "Ready?" he said, "I've gotta leave in 30 minutes, grandson's nativity." She nodded, ready yes but she had no clue about procedure. She breathed in the memory smells and sat expectantly in the squishy chair,

"Done this before?" No she had not, he jammed a pair of headphones over her ears, frowned and twiddled a few of the dials. Brendan sniffed, clearly irritated. "This 'as never 'appened before..." He poked and prodded, "Testing, testing – are ya there Mike?" but all was silence over the headphones, Liza noted the flickering dials which seemed to be wavering uncontrollably. Brendan fiddled some more, " 'ave to come back another time if I can't sort this," he said, grimly. As she looked, truth dawned on Liza, her dad was clearly putting in his six penn'orth. "Dad," she spoke aloud, "Dad, I know you couldn't resist being here but would you kindly not touch the dials? I know it looks like the stuff you used to work with but I think the tech's moved on by now..." As she spoke, she felt a glow of absolute recognition, a great flood of joy: her dad was there, supporting, proud.

Brendan gave her an odd look as all of the dials swam back into a functioning mode, Mike's voice came through as a tinny whisper on Liza's earphones: "You ready love? Just take your time, speak clearly and if you stumble, go back to the start of the sentence and start again. You'll be fine."

Liza took a deep breath and began to speak, "I don't own the perfect figure, I'm best described as a generous armful: a recent shopping expedition left me feeling that I am probably a very odd shape..." her words drifted like melting butter through the headphones as Mike, the producer captured the sound of her own voice.

12. The Soul of My Dog

They say, those people who profess to know, that animals do not have souls. That when we arrive at The Gate we'll be let in but there is a sign which expressly precludes all animals, in fact all things created except the superior being: Man. For this moment we'll ignore the idea that these Men must also have their lifetime passport stamped with the correct theory – imagine the discontented clunking of Viking warriors, the many followers of the god Mithras et al when they get there and discover they backed the wrong horse. Which of course brings me back to the subject of my supposing.

To my sadness, I have never owned a horse or even the tiniest pony, much less a sweet, cantering foal. At the present moment I own Monty – full name Montmorency Montague Moofish, aka Hector McFadyen. Even before I begin to introduce him fully, language trips me up. Is it possible that I, or anyone for the matter, can own any other creature? Own in the same way that we own a car, fountain pen, computer or bicycle? I have to contend with myself immediately, I can no more own Monty than he can invest in stocks and shares (though knowing his temperament as I do I think perhaps he does, but loses so heavily he keeps quiet about it). So, no, I think perhaps the term 'reside with' fits the situation far better.

He came into our lives when he was just nine weeks old, a small bundle of ginger fur with a rather large set of paws. On his way to our home, he expressed his nervousness by way of a wet fart and got covered in raggedy bits of shit. Hence his first introduction to our establishment was being lifted out of his cage by a pair of Marigold clad hands and into a sink of warm water. Cleansed, rinsed and dried, he curled up on my knee and fell fast asleep. I spent many of the following days thus seated, our small charge curled neatly in my arms, at my feet, or onto my hip as once my own children had been so curled. Feeling the warmth of this infant dog against my body brought a strong reminder of all the emotions evoked by motherhood, now so distant. This creature, utterly reliant on us for his care; unknown and slightly scary – we had never had a puppy before, what would he be?

One thing was certain, he would not, as our children have done, grow up, move away and live a life without need of us, an independent life to be part of which requires their permission. Monty would never reproach us with the outcomes of our clumsy efforts at parenting. The scars caused by doggy misunderstandings would be tangible rather than emotional. No, he would be our companion for the duration and ultimately we would always have the power of life and death over him.

When he first came to us, we wondered how well Monty would cope with separation from his mother. He was the last of a large litter and they were very used to each other. Bess had taught him well: there was no hint of distress on his part, Monty arrived and took his place in both home and heart as of right. We learned at a later date that the loss had been much harder on Bess who searched the house for him for many days after his departure, this knowledge tugging most guiltily on my heartstrings. He, on the other hand, walked about with an air of proprietorship which made us laugh. Monty told us, 'I'm happy to let the pair of you stay in my house, I trust you will obey the house rules, we'll see how you shape up.'

Prior to his acquisition we had discussed all of the boundaries he would never be allowed to cross, the idea that he would be fully aware of his place in the order of things. No feeding from the table, no extra treats of human food, no sitting on the furniture, no entry into our bedroom, definitely no access to our bed – on, in or by – at any point, no jumping up at visitors, running off: attention seeking behaviour would be ignored. Oh yes, we had it all worked out, we would be very strict because we did not want an out of control, smelly, badly behaved dog on our hands. Oh no, no, no....

In life there is always a massive gap between theory – like the chap who split the atom and was so aware of its potential for good – and reality, that same atom is used for good but also to obliterate the lives of countless people in the space of a few seconds. So the theory, this dog who would be perfectly behaved, the behaviour of any dog simply reflects the ability of its owner to control and the reality – in a word MONTY.

He is just over three years of age now, fully a part of our family. The thing we could not do, have human children as part of our union, was transmogrified in Monty – a form fantastic, a relationship bordering on the bizarre. A relationship so powerful, no matter what cynics may say about the motivation of food and shelter, that we have absorbed him into our lives and he has become a part of us.

The now of it all, the broken promises, about what and how, that we made to each other. The reality of Monty; he's sitting by me looking out of the balcony window. The spring sunshine is making his fur gleam bright as burnished brass, so many shades of red, yellow, brown and deepest orange radiate from him. Monty is a warm dog, he has numerous very human needs – warmth, food, shelter, care and exercise.

This last he needs almost more than any other making the relationship completely symbiotic. I cannot pull the quilt over my head on rainy or cold days as I would have done previously, the days will begin, come rain, come hail, come sunshine, snow, blizzard, tornado or hurricane. We've been early risers since our days in Zambia when daylight hours were restricted to twelve and nights could seem very long, we learned that every kind of light is precious. On a typical morning, we are woken initially by the early shipping forecast, that lyrical piece of un-poetry which is read in such a rhythmic, lilting way that it soothes the soul of even the most land-bound creature. I leave my eyes closed and drink in the music of the words, I lie in wait. Sometimes we snuggle our good-morning, limbs clustered, wound about so that we almost forget where one of us begins and the other ends. Eventually, one of us gets cramp and proposes a cup of tea: it's a bit of a 'who blinks first game'. Eventually one of us gives in and makes the ultimate sacrifice – to put your warm foot out of the warm bed onto the cold floor. The sound of the kettle's whistle is prefaced by the scrabbling of paws and claws: first as they move up the stairs, muffled by carpet and then as they pitter across the bare-wood bedroom floor. This sound is like the dropping of rice into a saucepan or the sound of hail against a windowpane. Sometimes, if he is unsure of which part of the bed is occupied, he will sneeze: a polite little sneeze like a courtesy cough. 'I am here, you know.' spoken in the fruity tones of a sophisticated doglet. And I say, 'Come on then,' and scratch the satiny surface of the bedding to indicate that he is welcome. The ritual continues with burrowing: I raise the upper end of the quilt, Monty dives nose first into the space and lies his full furry length against my legs, cold nose on bare legs, tail resting gently on my chin.

I marvel at this ability to stretch, to peg himself out, slim, long and lovely; I reach down and stroke his hindquarters. The tea arrives, a careful hand places the mug at the bedside with a muffled 'thunk'. I am aware that whilst not being intravenously administered, my tea is there, years of practise have taught me how to sip it from an almost horizontal position. All three of us sigh as my husband climbs back into bed and proceeds to warm his now very cold feet on Monty's fur. This is a moment of oneness, completeness, a time to be held ready in memory.

At this moment, I know that Richard knows that Monty knows that the triangle is complete. Sighs, farts, burps, mumbles, throat clearing, a small sneeze or a cough may break the silent communion we share but these 'hymns' to the start of the day complement the mood. Time stands still, we lie suspended, protected. At some point, one of us acknowledges the need to move, by motion rather than speech, one of us indicates that they will move and then all the im-motion translates into action.

The pattern of each day is similar: at the centre is Monty, we revolve around him and his needs. Our activities are informed and at times curtailed by him. This may sound like a tie but in fact it is a form of release, a grounding. Monty is our 'reason' – we must not be late, we must organise a dog-sitter, he will need to be fed, watered, stroked, cuddled, tucked up in his own bed. For those of you reading this who are about to vomit into your cornflakes, I ask you to suspend your cynicism for a while. Before Monty, we were free, before children, we were free in different ways their 'tying' fulfilled our needs. One of the most basic human needs is the need to be needed. Some speak of the empty nest syndrome, to me the feeling is a hollow in the heart. The children are gone, they have lives of their own which intersect with ours but on their terms. The rights of parenthood have been surrendered to their need for freedom, as a parent you must watch, wait, sense but never, never interfere, much less 'help' without invitation – more often than not, that invitation does not come, the apron string is broken. This is good, this is a necessary evolution, but the hollow that it leaves is never easy to live around. Permission to please yourself, to follow your own career, hobbies, to have absolute freedom to be loud, quiet, out, in – all of those permissions are yours to pursue. But for me, the hungry hollow remains.

The hardest part of being a mother was the transition from being the ultimate life support machine to being a stranger to the very people whose every inch of skin I knew so well. The womb which nurtured, the arms which held, the breasts which fed, the lap which comforted are empty. Life has become fulfilling in many different ways but the fulfillment I learned as the bearer of children cannot be repeated, nor can that memory be taken away.

Monty has become our perpetual child, he has taken his place in the hollow and made it his own.

Monty shows me that there is more, much more than I will ever understand with this human mind. He is now lying beneath the piano, legs comfortably, almost casually outstretched. My husband is playing the Bach prelude and fugue in F, Monty is listening, listening intently. Who knows what he is thinking, who knows what he is feeling? The relaxed smile on his face tells me that for him this is 'Bark' and the pleasures he takes from the music are his alone to know. When 'They' say animals have no souls, observing his sublimely lovely face at this moment confirms to me that 'They' are wrong. Within the mysterious sphere of creation, each and every thing created has a 'soul'. The Author of our universe, surprised by the joy of their own continuously evolving creation knows this, and has understanding far beyond our own human imagining.

13. The Fall

Celia lay in the grass. A minute or so ago she had been heading up Paper Mill Hill with her dog, Castro. Her rapid strides up the concrete steps pleased her, she felt she could move with ease and grace. Castro had pulled eagerly on the lead, they'd both appreciated the growing warmth of the sun and the stillness of this, the longest day of the year. Celia had been contemplating many things – Roman Soldiers with cold knees, the Solway Firth and why the Isle of Man was such a small dot on the horizon some days and so very much bigger on others, the meaning of life and whether it was worth it and finally what to make for pudding – it being Sunday, puddings were allowed.

Castro, on the other hand, was contemplating blades of grass, the subtle smell of urine pissed out by other dogs, the absolute right place to defecate (he was a most particular dog) and whether he might be able to sneak the Sunday Joint (sirloin of beef) off the kitchen work surface without anyone noticing.

It was at this point, two thirds of the way up the hill that Celia appeared to do a backward summersault, describing a wide but graceful arc in the air and landed with a resounding thud on the grass at the edge of the bank: Castro gave a yelp, sidestepped neatly, and narrowly avoided being crushed. It was a most spectacular not to say, unrehearsed, performance.

Celia contemplated the darkness, silence engulfed her. 'Am I dead?' she asked herself, reluctant to open her eyes and test the notion. 'If this is dead, I quite like it.' No more life, no more decisions, no more puddings, just a whole of eternity of nothing. She sighed deeply, mmmmm, if it's this simple, then the afterlife is for me. She felt a nothingness all around her, bliss, numinous, direct contact with other worlds. This last thought was an uncomfortable contrast to the concept of nothingness so she pushed it aside. She returned to the thought, 'If this is really dead, then I really don't much mind.'

Castro sat upright on the cold concrete step, a splinter of wood was sticking into his tail, he wriggled to make himself more comfortable. He waited...and waited...patiently. He thought to himself, 'Funny sort of place to take a nap. But then Celia can be a bit alfresco.' He looked around him, somewhere from one of the road side flats the smell of the previous night's barbecue lingered tantalisingly: he questioned the air with his nose, 'Mmmm... Pork ribs I think,' he sniffed again, '... probably farm bred and with plenty of bone...Mmmmm...eergh, yukkkk!' The scent of barbecue sauce filled his nostrils, 'I hate that stuff,' he thought, 'Ate some once by mistake and couldn't spit it out fast enough'. Castro laughed at the memory. The masticated meat bearing the offending sauce had landed in the cleavage of a young woman who was reclining close by. She'd had a tattoo of a thorny rose ascending from her left breast; the rose wobbled as she leapt up screaming, 'Whose bleeding dog is this?' Castro had moved away from her in dignified primness: a dog of his calibre could never tolerate such coarse language.

Celia drifted gracefully away on a cloud of nothingness – it was such a rare feeling, she did not want it to stop which, if this was eternity, she would never be obliged to do. Her brain seemed to slide in half and linger lovingly on a passing breeze – 'Goodbye brain' she thought. Then her arms took on a weight-free rubbery feeling – 'Ah,ha' she thought, 'Wings' and then she thought. 'No thank you, really no thank you. Please don't spoil eternity by giving me wings and I definitely don't want a harp – all that practising, no please: No wings, No harp.' Nothingness was enough – more than enough, she really, really, really did not mind.

Castro watched the man as he stood over Celia. 'Wonder if he's got any biscuits?' thought Castro. 'I could try giving him my Good Dog Smile – which can be quite winning - and see what happens. Then again, maybe I need to try out the Starving Dog Face, that's a winner too. Wonder what sort of bloke he is?' Castro looked the man up and then down, as far as he could tell the man was completely unaware of his presence on the path. 'Low growl? Polite cough? I'll try a sneeze, don't want to frighten him.' Castro sneezed, loudly, twice.

The man looked round, 'It's alright doggy, I'm here now, I'll take care of her.' DOGGY! Castro was deeply insulted, he had not been called doggy since he was a very small pup and that was by a horrible old lady who had a trailing cashmere shawl the texture of which had enlivened his senses, made him feel as though he was back in the womb. 'Please don't do that doggy,' she had said and tried to pull the shawl away, Castro, impressed by her desire to play, had tugged the shawl back – a game ensued which he mightily enjoyed but the old lady who had initiated it seemed to become increasingly agitated. Castro sniffed at the memory, some people just couldn't take losing, she'd stormed out of the house in a foul temper. Still, he'd won half of the shawl.

Celia sensed the shadow of the man standing over her. She did not want to move out of this space and kept her eyes firmly shut. 'If it is the Archangel Gabriel, he may well want an account of my life – I'm just not ready to give it. On the other hand he might want to fit me up with a regulation angel uniform and I wouldn't like that at all.' Celia had a dislike of angels dating back to the school play when she was five. Miss Stumbling had insisted Celia be an angel because of her 'lovely golden curls', (this spoken in a high pitched, I'm so nice to small children voice). Celia disliked the idea, she wanted to be one of the cows. Their costumes looked fun and they had twitchy brown ears made of velvet, they were lovely to stroke. Miss Stumbling had been unable to read Celia, she was so unlike the other little girls – didn't like dolls, often roughed it out in the playground with the boys. Celia didn't fit Miss Stumbling's 'girl mould' - sugar and spice and all of that malarky. She had taken the cardboard wings, they were sprayed with glittery stuff which to Celia's mind stank of wee, and waved them in front of Celia's face. 'There,' Miss Stumbling had said, ' Wings – so pretty dear, just let me slip them on.' Unable to make her teacher understand her refusal to wear the wings in any other way, Celia had taken a large bite out of the cardboard wings as they were wafted in front of her face: she then spat the bitten piece as far as she was able and had hit Gerry Sunderland in the eye. 'Shot,' she had thought to herself as he stood in stunned silence. The resulting punishment – being rulered across the back of her bare legs -only served to increase her resistance to 'wings' to become more deeply entrenched. She'd been made to sit with her mother for the duration of the nativity play and had stared resentfully at Gerry who wore one of the coveted cow costumes.

Castro had taken offence at the man now leaning over Celia's apparently inert body: he began to bark. What he was trying to say, but the stupid arse of a man would not stop to listen to him, was that Celia was merely taking a nap. Sometimes when they went walking she would lay in a field of grass staring up at the sky while he pottered about. Once she had removed all of her clothes and lain completely naked in a large patch of daisies: Castro had enjoyed that and rolled sympathetically in the grass beside her. He felt smug, his fur had protected him from the ants which rudely interrupted Celia's communion with nature. He'd thought, 'I tried to warn you but would you listen?' She'd leapt to her feet, slapping and scratching her skin, cursing loudly, fit to make a dog blush. It was only as she was replacing her clothes that Castro chose to make her aware of the farmer seated on a stationary tractor on the other side of the hedge eating his doorstep sandwiches.

Timmy stood over Celia's prone body: he was a sweaty looking individual in tight running gear, the pants of which defined rather too clearly his male status. He was in a dilemma, for as long as he could remember, almost the whole of his conscious life, Timmy had wanted to be a hero; few opportunities had presented themselves and even when they did, he had run away or been pushed aside by a more aggressive would-be hero. Timmy's body was frozen, if she were dead, he might be suspected but if she were not dead and he didn't try to resuscitate her, she might die anyway and then what? Manslaughter he supposed. He wrung his hands in a gesture which might have been interpreted as either prayer or despair, he muttered to himself 'What to do? What to do?' the three syllables forming a mantra on his lips.

Castro remained seated. He was uncertain of the man's intentions. He sat up on his haunches, raised his left leg to his ear and began scratching with vigour. Nothing like a good scratch when you couldn't think of anything else to do; except have a good bark, he pondered the concept of barking but it seemed rather too much trouble so he continued to scratch his ear.

Celia became aware that the apparent darkness was no longer still, there was a kind of bubbling around her for which she could not account. Within her darkened world she peered about seeking the source of the sensation: dozens of bubbles were floating around. Their rainbow translucence created light, lightness – holes of light in the black. She followed he movement of the bubbles and noticed that each one enclosed a small figure. 'Oh, they're me!' she smiled, reaching out a net of thoughts to catch them.

The mantra had a soothing effect on Timmy, he calmed and contemplated the situation. Experience had taught him that he had never once had the stamina to see heroism through to the end. A slight blush crept up his neck and over his ears as he thought about his friend Tom Gudgeon.

As a kid, Tom had dared Timmy to go scrumping at Mr Dean's allotment.
"It's easy," said 9-year-old Tom, "We just get down as flat as we can and crawl under the fence. Old Dean's got some really ripe apples – best I've ever tasted."

"Flat? Crawl? How, I'm not sure..." Timmy felt doubtful, afraid yet excited by the possibilities offered by this rebellion. But if his mother found out...

"You know, commando crawl – like on Blue Peter the other day."

Blue Peter was one of the limited number of programmes Timmy's mother permitted him to watch and always, just to be sure, she watched with him so that she could press the off button if any sight, thought or notion might not meet her very strict concept of what children should be exposed to. The only reason Timmy had been able to sneak an hour or so with Tom was because his mother had had one of her 'heads' and was resting in a darkened room. As far as she was concerned, Timmy was constructing an Airfix plane.

The commando crawl, as witnessed on Blue Peter had looked daring, easy. He had admired the camouflage garb as the soldier wriggled his body slowly but surely under a net, elbow swivelling over elbow.

'But what if...' Timmy began, uncertain that his mother's migraine would last long enough for him to complete the dare and get back into his bedroom safely.

'Bugger your what ifs,' snarled Tom, ' you up for the dare or not?'

In a moment, Timmy screwed all of his courage into one small ball, flung him self on the ground and began crawling. Suddenly his one desire was to pinch apples from Mr Deans and show that he wasn't 'yella' – an insult often fired at him in the playground.

Commando crawling was not quite the peace of cake it had looked, apart from anything else, his shorts and pullover got covered in mud and grass stains: he pushed aside the explanation he would have to give to his ever watchful mother and focused on the task in hand. Tom was well ahead of him, wriggling under the wire fence. Timmy felt exhilarated, the thrill of doing something so illicit, the thrill of doing something he would be able to boast about at school. He breathed a tight, deep breath and pulled his diaphragm as hollow as he could, sliding with ease beneath the fence. Half way under the fence, Timmy heard an ear-splitting scream, he looked across at Tom.

Timmy ran, ran and ran and ran as though his own life depended on it, as though the devil were pursuing him. He raced in through the back kitchen door and into his mother's arms. "What on earth..." She looked down at his soiled clothes, at his red, tearstained face. "Where have you been? Has something upset you? I thought..." the questions tumbled from her mouth as she held him close. Timmy wept, and as he wept he invented a story about a rose, high up over the wall, a rose he'd tried to pick for her the act of doing so had caused him to fall. Neither of them paid attention to the wail of the ambulance siren.

'Each one of those bubbles is me,' she contemplated them in wonder. Each rainbow, bobbing bubble was Celia, in miniature. 'So this must be the way past life flashes – not flashes at all.' The bubbles were perfectly round, and each one held Celia in its rainbow globe, showing her at different ages and stages. They drifted about her, bumping gently against her skin, cool as fresh peaches.

Castro looked across at Celia, her face was relaxed, euphoric, smiling but he also noted the tears seeping from beneath her eyelids. He walked over and licked them gently, they were salty and he rather liked salt. 'She's having a good long dream', he thought. 'Don't know what that fella thinks he's doing, he keeps standing there, rocking. I'd bark at him if I could be bothered.' Castro slumped down full length against Celia's side, the warmth of the rising sun was beginning to penetrate the day. 'I could lie here all day,' he sighed and closed his eyes. The summer had been a scorcher thus far and Castro had found it quite a strain. That was why Celia had brought him out early, so that they could both appreciate the cool of the morning, so that he could find a shady place to lie for the rest of the day. The dusty smell of dried grass wafted lazily into his nose he thought about the poodle with the pink collar. 'Bit of all right she was,' he sniffed savouring the memory of her. 'Small mind you, but quite nicely rounded. 'course we did the sniffing and licking routine: quite forward she was, she started it. If only I'd had me bits and she'd had hers, well just imagine.' He fell into a deep doggy sleep, his nose and eyes twitching, sometimes his legs running in dream, all was well in Castro's world.

Timmy saw the tears, "Must," he said aloud, "mean that she is still alive." So what next? He thought back to the First Aid course his company had required all of its employees to attend. A.B.C – yes, yes, that was it 'Airway, breathing, coronary.' Right. Now he'd decided, planning a course of action seemed to come naturally. 'The sequence? Yes, roll the woman onto her side, check her mouth for dentures and seaweed (no, no seaweed, she could not have drowned this far up a hillside), make sure she can breath, then check her pulse.' But what if there was no pulse? Was it mouth or chest first? Did you breathe and blow followed by press and push or was it the other way around? And what if he broke her ribs? He could make the plan, yes but what if? Then he saw the tears again and the flickering smile. 'People cannot smile and cry if their hearts have stopped!' he told himself firmly, stepping forward to touch the recumbent form.

'Here', thought Castro, 'What do you think you are up to?' from deep within his throat a nasty brown growl began to form. It was all very well for this idiot to stand there looking at Celia, but there was no way he was going to allow him to touch her. Castro, hackles bristling, stood up, ready to spring. "Look mate," he snarled, "one step further and I'll have your bloody..."

"You stupid fricking dog," shouted Timmy in fear, "can't you see I'm trying to help? Get out of the f...." The words faltered, Timmy was fearful that another step towards Celia might cost him his throat. He groaned, it was then that his mobile phone began to chirrup.

As Celia became increasingly aware of Castro's warning barks she also became aware, in the frequently used words on gravestones that she was 'Not dead but sleeping.' 'Such a shame,' she muttered as she resurfaced. A voice penetrated the receding mists: "A woman...yes...unconscious...no, there's a rather fierce dog..." Castro's roaring made her sit up, she stared nonplussed at the man in front of her. The sound of an ambulance siren penetrated her thoughts as a growing realisation dawned upon her addled brain...

14. A Summer's Lease

She brushed away the last few crumbs from the seat and was about to fold away her bedding when he approached her, diffidently, respectfully, "You can't do that here madam," soft-voiced, not wishing to offend.

Millicent smiled, her face as blissful as a freshly picked peach. "What is it that I can't do young man?" She patted creases out of the pink blue blanket, stowed it in a plastic bag and placed the parcel beneath the bench.

Rodge Trotter was dumbfounded. He'd been parks manager for Waverley Memorial Gardens for a little over twenty years, had turned out all kinds of vagabonds, vagrants, battled with the local 'youf' and generally managed to sustain the gardens as a place of dignified quiet. When he bellowed 'Keep of the grass!' he meant it.

Millicent coughed politely, "What is it that I can't do?" she repeated, "do tell me..." she waited, the smile on her serene face never wavering.

"You can't...you can't..." Rodge stammered, why was it so difficult enforce the regulations with this old duc?

"Yes?"...

"You can't camp here, it's against the rules you know..." finally he'd stammered it out, uncertain, a bit like a school boy stammering out the unconvincing reason why his homework was late.

Millicent's face assumed a puzzled expression. "I do see that," she said "but I'm not camping." All of the visual evidence seemed to contradict this statement and for once in his park keeper's empire, Rodge was nonplussed. He opened his mouth to speak but words failed him.

Millicent beamed, "I know what you need - the universal cure all..." She nodded her head encouragingly, "the cup that cheers. Do sit down and make yourself at home." She indicated the space next to her on the bench.

Rodge sat down in stupefied silence as Millicent drew a brass primus stove out from beneath the bench and emptied water from a bottle into a silver kettle. The pungent odour of methylated spirit scented the morning, the radiant warmth of the flame tickled up the chilly air: it was, after all, only seven o'clock of an April day, the sun was still a watery glow on the horizon.

"Biscuit?" Millicent's voice broke through Rodge's miasma. "They're Abbey Crunch, " Rodge sipped delicately from the bone china cup – Royal Doulton – and placed it carefully back in the saucer. His Gran had stuff like this but it was held in a secure glass cabinet on display. He brushed the biscuit crumbs from his stubbly chin, how to put it? Triplicate forms, Health & Safety... his boss's red face...his job on the line?

"Look," he said drawing in a deep breath before he spoke, "this is all very nice...a very nice cup of tea ...and the biscuits..." as he said this he wondered where she'd found them, he hadn't seen Abbey Crunch since Adam was a boy..."You can't camp here, I'm sorry but it's against all the regulations." There, he'd said it, surely she'd hear him now.

Millicent took his cup and placed it on the ground by her feet, "Thank you for your concern Mr..." she read the name from his badge, "Mr Trotter. I do appreciate that you have a job to do and I will confirm to your superiors, should they enquire, that you have done it." Rodge nodded his thanks and was about to speak but Millicent raised a hand to stay his words. "I want to assure you, Mr Trotter, that I am not camping here."

Rodge sighed, "The blanket?" he pointed to the mound of pink and blue, "...and the primus, the cups, the biscuits?" As he looked he became increasingly certain that he could see a powder blue toilet bag peeping out from one of the boxes beneath the bench. Another deep breath, another attempt to make her see reason, "Mrs...?"

"Call me Millicent, it is my name."

"Millicent, " he repeated trying to feel in charge of the situation. "Park regulations state that under no circumstances shall anyone be allowed to camp within the perimeter of the park: further, all visitors must vacate the park by sundown."

She nodded in response to his words, "Yes, yes I see." He waited but nothing more was forthcoming. Rodge was perplexed "I have to lock up you know..." Millicent nodded again "...so you understand then...Mrs er...Millicent, you CAN'T CAMP HERE." The last three words came out louder than he had intended, the effort of patience and keeping his temper was proving too much.

Millicent tapped his hand, made him face her, "I do understand and I want to reassure you that I'm not camping here. This..." she said, stroking the arm of the park bench, "...is my home."

...

Rodge felt punch drunk, to be outwitted by an old lady after all these years. What was she? Some sort of Hells' Granny? Maybe a strident senior citizen seeking her rights? She must be in the clutches of Dr Alzheimer, yes, he thought to himself, that's the answer. He'd contact Social Services, they'd have something to say about it.

...

Miriam Mbala, welfare officer for the elderly and confused, tripped along in the April sunshine. She was glad to have a case to sort out in the open air, she visited too many stuffy homes; sometimes the job felt claustrophobic. Ah yes, there was her confused client, bench number twenty-two. Sort this one out, really just a matter of getting hold of the relatives.

Millicent looked up and noted the approaching stranger, she was just casting off a needle full of stitches. She hoped the woman would take her time getting to the bench, it was all too easy to lose count these days. As the last loop slipped off the needle, Miriam pulled up level with the bench. "Hello," she smiled warmly, "you're Millicent?"

"Indeed I am – cup of tea?"

Mentally Miriam ticked off her list of points, the list she was obliged to follow when assessing the elderly and confused: Millicent scored a great big zero, she just didn't fit into any of the available categories. The only thing Miriam could pin on her was being elderly, that in itself need not be a problem: better dig deeper, "I am here to help you," she spoke calmly, reassuringly.

"That's very kind of you dear, now if you could just reach beneath the bench for the primus, I'll have the kettle on in a jiffy."

Miriam handed Millicent the primus, "When I said help...", Miriam bit into the Abbey Crunch – buttery, sugary childhood images flooded into her mind, she had not tasted them since her best friend's eighth birthday party, "...you see, the help I want to offer you is from social services. I mean, maybe you need help getting a home or carers or...well, what ever sort of help you might need."

Millicent poured boiling water into the pot and swashed it round, added the leaves and filled the pot to the brim with the rest of the freshly boiled water. "Would you prefer lemon or milk?" her voice was coloured by a firm but patient benevolence "It's very kind of you to be concerned, to offer help but I don't need any help. This is my home." She waved a hand over the bench and the surrounding area.

...

"She's right Rodge," Miriam caught up with Rodge Trotter just before leaving the park to find some lunch. "The park was given by the Waverley family to the people of this town: Millicent is one of its people."

"Rodge threw down his spade in despair, "Ms Mbala, you seem to forget the **REG-U-LATIONS!**"

"Well she's definitely not confused, she's fit... her mind is lively. She's got her little home sorted out... I for one favour leaving her to get on with it." Miriam adopted a 'case closed' visage and walked smartly away. Rodge shrugged his shoulders, picked up his spade and swore,

"...human rights." He muttered with a sniff. Maybe his wife could sort this out?

...

"...me and Rodge? Ooh...twenty three, no twenty four years Milly – we're very happy." Wendy Trotter beamed enthusiastically at Millicent. The Trotter's pint sized grandchild, Abel, pottered about on the grass with a dog on wheels happily nattering gobbledygook while Millicent and Wendy chatted nearly two hours away.

"It's time I was getting on, come on Abel my lad," she swept the boy onto her hip. "We'll put doggy in Gramp's shed." She turned to Millicent, "I'll be back tomorrow with some of that jam – thanks for the pickled herring recipe, Rodge will love that."

Millicent's eyes crinkled with pleasure, "Thank you Wendy, I've so enjoyed meeting you." She opened the biscuit tin, "Here Abel – bicky? That's right, one for each hand." Abel gurgled and grinned, the word 'doggy' was discernible within the jumble of sounds.

Wendy leaned over Millicent's diminutive figure, "You're all right you, and don't worry about old Grumpy Gramps – I'll put him straight." She kissed Millicent's powdery cheek and set off with the child and the wobbly-wheeled-dog.

...

"So what good did that do?" exploded poor Rodge over his egg and chips, "You were supposed to have made her see sense."

Wendy put an arm about his shoulders, "She has seen sense Rodge, that's why she's here. And I tell you, you won't move her in a hurry. Stop fretting lad, it'll work out."

Rodge groaned, "But Wendy the reg..." She stopped him short, "Forget 'em Rodge, they don't cover situations like this and she knows it."

...

The day had been a busy one for Millicent, her first day in a new home. Such a happy one bringing all the company she had hoped for. Rodge, Miriam, Wendy, Abel and then in the afternoon, homeward-bound children had stopped to talk to her. She snuggled down inside her arctic quality sleeping bag and watched the stars that night. This was a good move she thought as she drifted into sleep.

...

Thus the weeks passed. The flow of people stopping to tell her she couldn't do 'that there 'ere' ceased. Her residence in the park became an accepted fact of life, people came and went. Young mums came to confide in her about their troublesome toddlers and the difficulties of juggling home and career; older women came and said how much they admired her spirit. There had been a tricky moment when a gang of 'hoodies' had raced up to the bench on skateboards but Millicent had quietly diffused things. "How lovely of you to come, "she had said. "Perhaps you'd care for some biscuits?" Out came the Abbey Crunch: soon the boys, hoods down, were laughing with her; asking her about the games she'd played at their age. She shared especially happy memories of ice-skating on a frozen pond, long since concreted over. "... it was the gliding I enjoyed the most, it almost felt like flying."

A sandy haired lad with a cheeky grin suddenly said, "Hey, Gran, why don't you have a go?"

Millicent looked at him thoughtfully, "Well, do you know, I rather think I would like that." Gentle as a basket of eggs, three of the lads helped her onto the skateboard whilst a fourth held it still. They gripped Millicent firmly as they pushed the board along the tarmac pathway: all of them were laughing fit to burst.

Over the top of the laughter boomed Rodge's voice, "No skateboarding on the pathways. Kindly use the designated area." Then he saw the culprit at the centre of the group, tutted and raised his eyes heavenward. He might just as well rip the rulebook up: it had to be said the old girl had plenty of life in her and by being there she brought life to the park.

...

Throughout the warm summer days, Millicent lived to the rhythms of nature, waking with the birds and resting beneath the moon. Her daily routines varied little.

On Midsummer's Eve she was awakened by the sounds and movements of a group of revellers dressed in highly coloured garb. She observed them as the circled a flowerbed and danced rhythmically round dahlias, pelargonium, pansies and old roses. They chanted quietly, the moon silvered their faces, gave them an ethereal beauty. Millicent sighed, she was tired, wished it were not so – she would have liked to join the dance. When she woke at dawn, a single white daisy lay on top of her sleeping bag, the day felt fresh and new.

...

September the first came in the blink of an eye, summer's song changed to a subtle, gradual valedictory. Miriam Mbala, one of Millicent's favourite visitors, sat with her over a cup of Lady Grey. "The weather will soon turn Milly, it's time for you to think about moving on," Miriam said, as kindly as she knew how.

Millicent smiled at her, munching placidly on the last of the Abbey Crunch, "Don't trouble yourself my dear, I know my next move."

"That reassures me," responded Miriam hoping to learn more but knowing better than to press things. The old lady had been in control all along, there was no reason to doubt her now. "May I bring Mrs Cartwright to visit tomorrow? She does enjoy the park." Millicent's peaceful persona helped to calm Mrs C, she could fully appreciate and comprehend Mrs C's ramblings about 'the old days'.

"You do know," Miriam mused, "that you've cast a spell here. It's a unique sort of social service in a world that was too busy to know it needed you."

"Thank you Miriam. My mother taught me that in this life we must always be of service." Then Miriam did something she had always been a little too awed to do before: she embraced Millicent, the peachy cheek brushing her own with warmth, with love.

...

"The park was given by the Waverley family to the people of this town: Millicent is one of its people."
Miriam's words were true: and despite being the Waverley heiress, Millicent was one of the people of the town. It was loneliness that had inspired her to take up residence on the bench.

She woke before just before dawn on September the fourth, bathing in glorious thoughts of her companionable summer. The scent of autumn, the crispness of change was all about her.
A young man approached her, he was bathed in the pink light of morning,
"You can't stay here, " he smiled.
"I know," she said taking his hand.
...

Rodge always visited Millicent's bench first thing after he'd opened the park gates for the day and it was then he found her. Her summer's lease was at an end: Millicent's final sleep was deep and easy.

15. Fog

It wasn't until later that I began to realise what had happened to the earring back: it was when I opened the fridge and found my glasses staring back at me. They were placed very neatly on top of a bar of soap. The block of cheese was sitting tidily in the soap dish.

You are almost certainly saying to yourself 'Dementia'. It isn't. I've always been absent minded, it's part of my personality. When my children were small we loved to walk down to the village pond to feed the ducks…

…Don't you agree that ducks are the most beautiful shade of green? It's a sheen that reflects in the sunlight, translucent, shimmery. I liked to point these things out to my babies and they, in their turn enjoyed feeding the ducks. A win win situation really. On this occasion the day was frosty and the sun was out, blessing the trees and the grass with its beams. It was cold, very cold, but dry – frost always gives me that sharp feeling that every kind of mental cobweb is being iced away. We stopped by the hedges to look at the cobwebs. So much enchantment in the spider's lace home: when silvered with frost, the magic is complete. We took some green twigs, bent them and caught the glistening webs. If you raise the frosty web to the skyward the delicate filigree is lit by the sun. Nature's artistry at its most subtle. My 3-year-old son wafted his twig on the air and watched it billow slightly: he let go of the twig, it pinged back into the hedge.

The pond reflected the sharp blue of the sky, little clouds scudded above our heads and at our feet. And there were the ducks. They knew we would come, we visited at much the same time each day - after Bobby's feed and when Terry was becoming restless for fresh air. Bobby was snuggled close to my heart in a baby sling – a relatively new concept in the days when my boys were babies. I'd load him up once he'd been fed and changed and he would sleep contentedly until the next time hunger struck. Terry held my hand tightly as I sought the bread; I pulled the bag out and handed it to him. The ducks waddled closer, eager to have their fill. Terry looked at me with that quizzical gaze small children have when life gets a bit confusing. "Are the ducks poorly mum?"...

...I do so love to see the world from a small child's perspective. It seems to me remarkable that the majority grow up and integrate into society with such consummate ease. Sadly, most children do that at the cost of an inquiring mind, a limitless imagination. Recently, Terry's own three-year-old son came to stay. "Nan," he said, "can I watch you scrub?" "Of course," I responded curious to know what this might lead to. I got out my toothbrush and the lad looked at it and said, "I think I'll use that today." I explained that toothbrushes are not things you let other people use. He raised an eyebrow and said sternly, "Nan, you must share."...

...On this particular day, it was my son Terry doing the puzzling, he repeated, urgently needing an answer to his dilemma, "Mum, are the ducks poorly?" In those days, medicine bottles were taken back to the chemist for reuse. It wasn't recycling which I think is perhaps a relatively modern concept: it's what I'd call not wasting stuff. I looked down at the bag Terry held in his hand, I saw the cause of his confusion: he was holding a bag full of pill bottles, brown, glass and empty, ready for us to take to the chemist. Strange because I'd dropped the pill bottle bag in earlier. You can guess the rest, and no I didn't get the bread back so the ducks went hungry that day...

Where did I begin? That's the trouble, I can so easily be side tracked, or fall into a total dwaal these days. I don't mind too much. The most frustrating part is that I've lost the knack of multi-tasking. You know the sort of thing: clean the kitchen while baking a cake, reading a story to the children, playing a game of Snap and arranging how to pay off mortgage arrears. But these days, I have to operate within a one-task mind. I have a blue book, an old style exercise book; each day I write down what I need to do, what I ought to do and what I'd like to do. I work through each point, sometimes not completing as my body winds down before I get to the end. I need my blue book because some days I feel that I've done nothing but crash out with a hot water bottle under the duvet. With the blue book, I can at least tick off what I have achieved.

Oh yes, the earring back. I rather think I swallowed it. The thing is that I have one of those medication boxes which you fill up with pills to last seven days. I refused the pink one – they are for really old ladies. The one I possess is a sickly green, the sort of green they used to paint on toilet walls. I was changing my earrings ready to go to the wedding of a nephew when I realised that I'd nothing to put my studs in. It occurred to me that putting them in one of the empty compartments would mean I'd find them later, or sometime when I topped up the box. I got very tired at the wedding, although I did enjoy the event: unusual for me, I prefer funerals as you always know the outcome. So it was with a foggy head that I took my pills and then couldn't find the earring back.

You see, I'm just fifty-nine, not an old lady at all. My life has been taken over by something they call 'Fibrofog' which is an aspect of something they call Fibromyalgia. Some days it feels as though I'm trying to live with my head in an opaque, plastic bucket. I try to look through it, my sight is dimmed, I try to hear through it, my hearing is dull. It can't be helped so there's not much point being sad and some of the mix-ups can be amusing.

You may see me, or someone like me – in a café say, looking glazed and somewhat detached. I may ask you what day it is, or the name of the town, or the name of the café: I may not be able to bring to mind the name of the drink I want – the glaze will be me searching for the right word. Or maybe I'm that person in the supermarket, blocking up the aisle as I try to remember what the heck I came in for: I will probably be talking to myself: "Now what was it? Shampoo? Dog food? Pickled herrings, yes that's what it...oh that butter looks expensive. It wasn't butter but you know when I was a kid they said that if we went into the Common Market butter would be ten bob a pound! If I could find butter at 50p for 500grams I'd be delighted! That door's alarmed, oh dear, I wonder what upset it?" I will probably chuckle a bit and then move on, my brain having found the unwritten 'shopping list'. Please don't be cross with me. Stop and chat about the weather or give me a wide berth if you think I'm barmy, but don't be cross: it's only fog.

(**For quite a long time now I have lived with a peculiar state of mind and body which has now been diagnosed as Fibromyalgia (FMS) – it won't kill me but it's changed my life forever. One friend could not get the name right – "Sounds like Aggie," she said. Thus Auntie Aggie personifies FMS for me: a very troublesome relative who has moved in permanently. If I treat her right, she'll grumble quietly in a corner, but if I forget she's there, she'll play merry hell. 'Fog' is dedicated to her.)

16.The Naming Of Dogs

After a great deal of careful, grown up thought we decided that we should like to own a dog: the fact that the dog now owns us is something for discussion at a later date – or possibly never.

'He' was one of a large litter of Patterdales and the choice was too difficult. We went to 'choose' and were told we could have second pick from the last three dogs as a family was travelling up from Lancashire and they had phoned first. In a way, I am very glad that family was coming because it meant we had to number the pups in order of preference. Imagine them, 4 weeks old, mewling and squeaking and little bigger than my hand. My first feeling was that we should take all three as it would be a shame to take a solo, it would be lonely. Tom, my partner, wise to this one shook his head firmly. Reasonable I suppose but a shame, I did not try to press the point. But which to choose?

Mum was a petite black lady with a kind face. She was gentle with her pups, did not seem to mind us handling them, which seemed to be a good sign. Dad was off the scene but as Bess was a family pet, we took him on trust. The first one I held was a quivering bundle of black, silky fur. He had the typical Patterdale trade mark – a white flash on his chest, he snuggled up to me, he was warm, he fit my space to sheer perfection: he was the one. Except that I had not considered the other two.

I put 'Blackie' down in favour of 'Brownie'. This second doggy pup was melted chocolate brown, his coat just as silky as his brother's: I looked into his face and saw him asking, 'Choose me'. I could see that this would be the perfect choice, sweet nature, on the bashful side, liquid chocolate eyes and a well-shaped face. How tiny his legs were, he only just fitted into the crook of my arm. Yes, Brownie would make a lovely family pet, we'd enjoy having him around. But then there was…

Well how can I describe dog three? By contrast with his brothers, his coat was as wiry as a yard broom, his legs were long and his feet were large. Whereas the other two, had a certain poise and decorum, this third one lacked finesse. We had, in all fairness to consider him. So down went Brownie and up came 'Wiry'. Whereas Brownie and Blackie clung near to Bess, 'Wiry' strode round the room as though he owned the place. He stretched out his back and looked at us in a proprietorial way, 'Hello,' he seemed to say, 'I AM ME – who are you?' Wiry did not mind being held, though he did not seem to form the same neat ball as his siblings.

So which one to choose? Blackie was nice, Brownie was sweet, Wiry was...Wiry had … personality. Did we want a dog with personality? Well, yes... no... but sort of, well maybe... Order of preference? We absolutely definitely decided that it was Brownie, then Blackie, then Wiry. Then we reconsidered and decided that it must be Blackie, then Brownie then Wiry... Then we decided, we decided we simply could not decide. Two other families were coming to see the pups, both families had children so the best option seemed to be to leave it to fate. Which we did and got – Wiry...

I wasn't actually that pleased, part of me wished we had stated our preference not to take him but by then it was too late. It was obvious that he was what people call a character and that we would have to live with the consequences of leaving choice to chance. However, his name was not something I was prepared to leave to chance.

If it was difficult to choose a pup, a name is well nigh impossible. I rather liked the name Small (as in Winnie the Pooh) but the paws indicated that this might well be an ironic name. Tiddles would be fun but humiliating as it is normally a name given to cats: I don't think they much like it either. We sat one night preparing to receive 'Wiry' – he certainly could not be called that, it would be plain ridiculous. A large piece of A3 paper was taped to the table, we'd do the thing properly. Coloured pens at the ready, we began to scribble. Tom wrote at speed, it seemed that one name tripped off his pen after another. At the end of an hour I had written just three names in luminous pink and Tom had covered the entire sheet. We stood back to admire our handiwork. The names I had written were, Alphie, Snubs and John. Tom sniggered. I threw my pen on the table and started to look at his choices.

Tom the wonder-dog-namer had written variations on just one name: that of Ronnie Biggs. Now I don't know about you but I do not think it a good start for a small, innocent pup to be named after a notorious criminal. What on earth was Tom thinking of? He'd been a child when the Great Train robbery had happened, he'd always been fascinated with the tale. Biggs was one of his heroes. HEROES, I shouted at him, how could that be? That fellow was an evil, manipulative... no, no said Tom, clever, articulate and he almost got away with it... Got away with it? I was full of moral outrage and told him so. The ensuing heated discussion (for which read one god almighty row) ended at bedtime when, as per tradition we slept in separate rooms. Not to worry, this is our way of dealing with upsets: kissing and making up the following day is always... interesting.

Next morning over toast and marmalade we discussed the dilemma, it seemed that choosing a name for the new arrival was more loaded and infinitely more complex than choosing a name for a child. Tom tried to tempt me with Biggles, which I liked as it made me think of the new puppy wearing flying goggles and a leather jacket: then I noticed that this was one of the variations on the R Biggs selection and refused to discuss the idea any further. What was wrong with my suggestions? Tom snorted with barely concealed contempt: Alphie was too much like alpha and the dog would think he was in charge, Snubs wasn't even worth talking about and as for John? Well, first of all no one ever calls their dogs John and in any case, he said rather quietly, he'd been bullied by a boy at school called John. At that point I went quiet myself and changed the subject.

We spent the next twenty-four hours being very polite to each other and the politeness ended with a phone call from his six year old niece, Clara. I say six but in many ways, she is going on for sixteen and rather scary. I heard Tom telling her about the new puppy, her squeals of delight were evident from across the room, followed by enquiries about when she'd be able to come and visit and, as a matter of course, what the pup's name would be. Ah, I heard Tom say, well that's the snag... Clara let forth a volley of ideas which had Tom rocking with laughter. I had my usual chat with her and told her more about the pup. After I put the phone down Tom looked at me with his 'I have an idea face': how about asking Clara to name him? I pulled a face, what ideas has she had – you laughed so much they must have been absurd. He mentioned 'Plop Face', 'Sloopy Draws' and 'Mylie Cyrus' – happily we agreed that not one was suitable.

Peace broke out over the next few days and we'd fire names at each other, unexpectedly but not a one fitted poor old 'Wiry'. He could not be Wiry, too much like Willy; 'Rough?' – unimaginative; 'Napoleon?', far too dominating and likely to be shortened to 'Nappy'.

Suddenly, like the proverbial bolt, inspiration struck. I was reading one of my trashy-head-holiday novels and bemoaning the lack of style and subtlety when Tom sprang to his feet with THE ANSWER! An answer which appealed to us both. Why not make a short list of authors' names and let Clara choose one of those? After a very brief tussle, we were tiring of the subject by now, we settled on the following: Charlie, for Charles Dickens; Robbie, for Robbie Burns; Walter, for Walter Scott; Bill, for W.Shakespeare; and finally Monty for Montmorency out of Three Men in a Boat.

There was a tense moment as we proposed the list to Clara, which would she choose? She hovered around

Walter, considered Robbie for five minutes and then settled on Monty. Problem solved, absolutely, that is until Monty made himself fully known to us.

As time passes I find he has a full set of pretty grand names. To the common herd he is known as Monty and, when not suffering selective hearing loss, answers to this especially when coupled with the word, 'biscuit'. In private, he informed me with great ceremony of his full title (which if he ever chooses to acknowledge the Kennel Club and allow them to have him as a member he will insist in full). His name, he explained, is actually Montmorency Montague Moofish, very fine it is too. Then in a moment of Masonic communication he informed me that his private name, only to be used under licence is Hector Mc Fadyean. The Masonic bit figures completely, as he leads me to believe he is a reincarnation of Edward VII – who was featured in full flig on the front of a cigar box. He doesn't like to talk about his former life and puts his paws over his ears at the merest hint of Queen Victoria's name. (He won't even watch East Enders).

I realise now that the matter of Monty's name was settled without us needing to worry or fight at all. He knew who he was from the start, he just didn't tell us.

17. The Earwig

I'm there ratching through the sale rail of women's underwear, elbow to elbow with all of the other bargain hunters. In my hands I hold a pair of magenta knickers with a Betty Boop logo and I'm wondering whether my husband might like them: they are just £10, they've got a Basking Shark label... and full price they were, well let's just say I'd never have even considered... But it's then I hear them and mechanically, Betty Boop falls from my fingers to be retrieved by whom I know not.
"...it was," says the large lady in the maroon jacket (with Peter Pan collar)..."as big as a two pound coin and bright orange". When she says the words 'bright orange' her voice drops to that confidential sort of a whisper people adopt when they don't want anyone to hear. I duck underneath the sale rail, knocking down a few rather nasty alleged designer jackets as I push through: I need to hear.

I pursue the speakers, keeping my eyes fixed on the companion, contrastingly thin as a drainpipe and about six feet tall. That's good because it makes them easy to spot. They pause to look at a display of rather obviously sexy underwear: I ponder which of them might choose it then browse as closely as I can. I've got a red lace corset in my hands now, could anybody wear that and still be able to breath? I'm as close as I can get, I tune my ears in, relieved to have caught up with them. Through pursed lips Maroon jacket hisses, "I've said he'll have get it took off. I mean to say, it's not reasonable." Drain Pipe responds with a nod of her head, lowers her eyes "I tell you I'd feel exactly the same: if it were me I'd say, I would say..." caught up in the drama of her thoughts Drain Pipe's voice rises to emphasise her point "...Lance it! Root it out." Unexpectedly, the pair of them walk rapidly away and are through the exit. I try to follow but I still have the flipping corset in my hands and am forced to go and put it back.

I'm dying of curiosity, it's unrequited: what on earth could be bright orange and as big as a two pound coin? I puzzle as I stand in the queue for coffee. It needed to be lanced? Was Drain Pipe speaking figuratively or was this some rare and ghastly form of tropical disease? Could it have been a feature obelisk that had gone wrong? That's the trouble with my hobby, it's only infrequently that I get to hear the end of the conversation and on the rare occasions when I do, the solution is mostly banal.

My hobby. Oh sorry, I forgot to explain, I'm an eavesdropper, an earwigger, a nosey parker. If you caught me out you'd probably give me a hard stare, perhaps even tell me to mind my own business; or, as on more than one occasion, tell me to **"****off"**. Well, I must say I dislike language like that and I say so, I mean no harm - it's not as if I do anything with the information. Every body ought to have a hobby, I'm not into pumping iron, mountain biking, yoga or amateur dramatics: I do not like baking, the current search for the perfect Victoria Sponge leaves me cold. As for phone-ins – they're just an excuse for people to sound off about their own special choice of bigotry. No, I listen in to other people's conversations.

You might wonder how I got into it. It's quite simple really, I'd been retired a few months, I didn't feel so good. I'd cleaned the windows 'til the glass nearly wore through, shampooed the carpets to death and picked all the fleas off our Peke. The curtains had been washed, ironed and re-hung. To be honest the house began to smell like a chemical weapons factory and Derek, my husband, started to get annoyed. "Will you calm down Marjorie?" he said angrily as he walked off to the Queen's Head for a pint taking the Peke with him. I think he guessed I was about to give his coat a going over… again. I can tell you, I sat down and wept. You hear about folk who go doohla' after they retire, I began to think I was one of them, or even that I might have that C.O.D. thing – you know the one I mean where you can't stop - I saw about that on the telly, people go on e-bay in the middle of the night. No, I think I've got that a bit muddled but you know what I mean. I went and had a bath, a long hot one with plenty of bubbles, sod the water meter. Far from cheering me up, the bath just made me feel really down, unusual that because it's my chosen therapy for most ills. I made hot cocoa, but I couldn't stop crying: I had to throw it down the sink, it tasted salty.

It was at that moment that Derek came back, caught me round the waist as I stood at the sink. "Sorry love," he said, planting a kiss on the back of my neck. Pringle the Peke started barking, he does that, he's always been a bit jealous. We both laughed and told him to shut up, which he didn't. Derek said, "You smell nice," he said it so tenderly it started me off again, I just could not stop.

I went on like that for a few days, the house was already so clean it made no difference that I stopped cleaning, cooking and washing. After a week, when I'd just moped about and watched enough daytime TV. to suffocate a dead man, Derek brought me the most beautiful bouquet of spring flowers and said, "I think you need to talk to someone love." Very direct he is, Derek, he was the one who picked up the phone and got me an appointment. I wasn't keen but the young lass I spoke to (she looked no more than 14 but the badge she wore said 'Doctor' so I suppose she must have been qualified) was so kind. She talked about the bereavement people feel when they make major changes in their lives. She asked me if retirement had been my choice? Well it was, the firm was offering a decent redundancy package, being three years off retirement age anyway, I was in pole position to get out. Which, frankly, I was glad to because they were making radical changes to the systems and I just didn't feel I'd be able to get my head round any more new information. So, yes, I was glad to go. But as the lass pointed out: mine had not been a planned decision. She was right of course. I must say for such a young woman she seemed to be so well informed, so very sympathetic. We talked about her Mam who'd been in a similar position to me. We talked about how she'd coped: I think I'd like to have met her Mam but of course that wouldn't be possible, it'd be a breach of the hypocritical promise they make. Her Mam had taken up macramé. Not my cup of tea, all those knots and nothing to tie up but it got me thinking. A hobby.

My hobby was born as I waited at the chemist to cash the prescription the lass had given me to help me get back on top. She felt, and I agreed with her, that a spot of help from a few pills would get me to the start line. Waiting, with the most miserable faces I've seen in many a day, was a young couple. She had a tattoo of a butterfly underneath her right eye, her face was full of piercings: like a pincushion in a traffic jam. He wore torn jeans, his hair was stiff with lacquer, all spiky bits and rainbows. I crossed to the shelves behind them and started to look at the range of denture fixatives: I don't have dentures, my teeth are all my own, but the patterns on the boxes caught my eye. I was just looking at the price of one box, £7.20, which I thought a bit steep, when I heard him mutter, "...but the handcuffs chaffed my wrists." I was all ears, had he been arrested? She laughed! " I told you, you should have used the baby oil. In any case it serves you right, the way you used that turkey-baster was actually quite painful." They both sniggered. I thought about it all the way home: turkey-baster? handcuffs? baby oil? What could it mean?

I got buried so deep in my thoughts that I forgot where I was going and before I knew it I was in the local supermarket with my antennae buzzing: a thousand and one fragments of conversation, all there for me to tune in to, all for free.

I marvel at the wonders of other people's lives, the patchwork, the tapestry of it all. "...and when I saw what George had in his hand..." I observe the mouths closely, how they contort, how the eyebrows rise in horror, surprise or simply in the form of a question mark. "...all, ALL, I say taken away..." "Of course she wanted a villa in Madeira but he, well you know what he was after..." "...and then I yelled **GET YOUR BLOODY HEAD out of my**

lavatory…" "…plans must be very well timed…" "You could tell what had happened, there was a large amount of coconut spilled on the carpet." And so on. I'm addicted, I've got a hobby which gets me out of the house, has widened my education – I always wondered what was meant by a blow job but never liked to ask, I've discovered the difference between walking the dog and dogging: I've even found out how to pot on my violets.

So the thing is, I have two things to end with. First of all, no one is obliged to go down the traditional arts and sports paths – so passé – find a hobby that really makes your heart race. Second, if you should see an older sort of lady with a look of intense concentration on her face – she may be holding an unlikely combination of items, perhaps a kipper clipper and a purple toilet brush – if you see this lady it will only be me trying to tune into some extraordinary or bizarre conversation: don't be alarmed. And please, don't mumble.

18. Silver Shoes

In our village the Brownie pack met every week in the school. We danced around a large, brown papier-mâché mushroom. 'We're the Brownies here's our aim, lend a hand and play the game' we sang as we danced. Each Brownie Pack had sub-teams – were they called patrols? I forget. I was a Fairy, but there were Gnomes and Pixies and Elves – each one with its only little song, all designed to inculcate a sense of personal responsibility. I could never tie knots, found it hard to remember how to light a fire and was ultimately quietly 'expelled' to the guides with my friend Kate when we got too old and too boisterous. I can't remember what we did that was so bad, but there we are; some past misdemeanours it's probably best to forget.

There were so many things I loved about being a Brownie. Strangely, one of them was being allowed to return to school in the evening when it was not school: the classroom had been transformed into a home for Brownies. I loved the dance around the mushroom, the singing around an imaginary campfire and the stories told by Brown Owl. Sometimes we got outside into the playground to make real campfires and the toasted marshmallows, burning our tongues and fingers. It's hard to believe, looking back after so many years that an ash-coated, melting sugary mess could be so desirable.

Then there was 'Bob-A-Job'. We'd go around in teams of two or three, knocking on doors – we'd been allocated a street - and ask if there were any jobs we could do. One of the loveliest memories I treasure is of the lady in a double fronted 30's house - it had bow windows. Now she saved her brass coalscuttle for us each year. Kate and I would sit on either side of a newspaper-covered-hearth-rug and polish using wads of Brasso soaked rags. We'd laugh so much as we rolled the scuttle between us, polishing and pretending to be Scottish. It was a great way to spend an hour: not only did we earn our 'bob' for the pack but we were given delicious refreshments which included the height of Epicurean indulgence – Jacobs Chocolate biscuits, each in its own individual wrapper. Unbelievable, hedonistic pleasure for children whose nearest approach to indulgence was six pennyworth of broken biscuits.

Knots, campfires, bob-a-job – fun though they were , they paled into insignificance when compared with a jumble sale. I do not recall how often they happened in the village, they were always a popular way of raising funds, and when we did them for the Brownies, we got to do the collecting. Door after door we'd knock on: have you any jumble for the Brownies? A few people were a bit short, said 'No' and shut the door but the majority were so good hearted. Some even had bags of stuff ready for us to take. It's the smiles of welcome I remember and the waft of the tea cooking which might escape through the door. The homely smells of newly washed lettuce or a freshly baked pie; the sweet smell of bread and butter or cake. Do you know, some of those people were so posh they got bought cake in a box from the Co-op? I envied them, we just had the homemade stuff my mother cooked. Then there were the bags and boxes which we'd carry between us up to the old Nissan hut which had been turned into a W.I. hall. Smells? That hall smelled of damp sawdust, mains gas and mothballs. A delicious combination. I always wondered what it would be like to live there. It had a stage where my mum and her W.I. pals would act out their annual drama, on either side of the stage were the dressing rooms full of old costumes. I thought it would be nice to use the stage as a living room and wear the clothes from the dressing room. There were very basic toilets, partitioned in wood and closed with massive black iron bolts. I don't think I ever got as far as thinking about other practicalities like eating drinking and sleeping but then children never do.

When we got to the hall with our treasure hauls, it would be dumped in a huge pile in the middle. And we got to sort it! In those days you didn't worry about health and safety types of things. Looking back I can't imagine what horrors some of those bag must have held by way of sharp, rusty objects not to mention a quota of unwashed clothing. It did not matter, to the best of my belief not one of us came to harm. We'd hold up dresses from different eras – the 'retro merchants' would go mad for the stuff now. Some of the ornaments were exquisite, some just downright ugly; the kitchen equipment was usually pretty battered – chipped enamel or dull aluminium – but it would do someone a good turn and if not, the Rag and Bone Man would benefit at the end of the sale. Everything was sorted into piles, boys clothes, girls clothes, baby clothes, clothes for women, clothes for men. Then there was the kitchen stuff and the books but favourite of all there was the White Elephant Stall. Heaped on, under and by the table were treasures from the aforementioned ornaments to cranky sets of dining chairs, hand mowers, jewellery and garden stuff. For some reason shoes were sold from this table as well.

Once the sale commenced, "Don't open those doors a minute before two o'clock!" Brown Owl would remind us, the women flocked in complete with capacious shopping bags, sharp elbows and rude tongues. The noise was deafening. The stalls were not staffed by Brownies: the rude women would have made mincemeat of us. We made the tea on a rota basis filling massive teapots from terrifyingly hot kettles, lifted from an old gas stove which was infinitely too high for us to reach. And yet we did it, not a one of us got more than splashed.

The best part of the jumble was your time off, the moment when you got to spend the coins jingling in your pocket. I did love the old money, it felt real. The solid coppers – I'd search for lucky 'Bun Pennies' – a twelve sided three-penny bit would rotate satisfyingly round in my fingers as I thought about what I'd like to buy and sometimes, sometimes I might even have a slender, silver sixpence. Treasure indeed!

When it came to my turn I'd drift round the stalls in a day dream watching the women as they bartered, argued and laughed: it was always good natured even when things got a bit rowdy about prices and correct change. It felt like being part of a massive, raucous family: familiar, safe and full of rough love. After a bit, I'd head to the bookstall. Two books stand out in my mind, sadly I no longer possess them. One was a book of short stories by Enid Blyton: 'The Red Spotted Handkerchief', the other 'The King Who couldn't Stop Sneezing' – by whom I really cannot recall.

Finally the White Elephant Stall with its eccentric array of items beckoned me. Having been part of the sorting I knew what many of them were, but there were always extras, things never seen before. Quite beyond my reach were the musky smelling tortoiseshell dressing table sets – if only I'd had a kidney shaped dressing table and the one and nine asked for the prettiest of the sets. I've learned that wishing for things is generally much better than achieving them, that's taken a very long time, but still the memory of those so unattainable objects brings me pleasure. I might not have been able to have them but no one could stop me dreaming.

What attracted me to spend a whole sixpence on a white china nude about five inches high? She had real hair. The glaze was matt but the china was smooth, pleasing to the touch: the hair, dark and coarse. The face and body were featureless, there was nothing explicit about the body. Memory bounds in with a glitzy flash of silver - a pair of strappy 1920's shoes. I did not want to wear them I just wanted to own them. They shone out at me, calling me to spend three pennies on them. I wonder now where they came from, whether a flapper had danced the Charleston in them, elegant cigarette holder in hand – these are things I wonder, now with an adult perspective. I can see the colour, smell the sweaty leather, but I cannot bring to mind the reason they seemed so desirable. They just were.

What happened to those shoes, those books, that figure? All gone but what remains in my mind's eye is the magic of the silver shoes which once, for so short a time, belonged to me.

19. What She Really Thinks...

"... and they come here thinking that because they've paid £30 for a single night's stay they own every part of you. I wouldn't have them here if it wasn't for the money. Not a penny did the old fool leave me, what with his gambling and his booze, not a single penny if it weren't for these four walls, I'd have nothing: and what a state they were in I can tell you. The only thing I had after he carked it was this place; this damned cottage in the middle of nowhere with an overview of sheep, pasture, hills and more bloody sheep. Doesn't matter which direction you look in, there are sheep and greenery and trees. They come and they wax all poetic about it, 'Oh my dear but you must have a beautiful soul living so close to nature – a thousand shades of green...' then they come over all reverential and stare, and stare until I wonder if they're having some kind of fit, but before I decide to call an ambulance they suddenly come too with tears in their eyes, they rest a hand on my elbow, sigh and walk away: it takes them like that this place.

'course you're wondering why, how what and where? Nosy like the rest but never mind, I'll tell you since you don't own me and you aren't staying. £30 a night does not buy my soul: it buys my arsehole, figuratively speaking that is. I work my backside off to keep the place running, to keep a place people want to come back to, to recommend to their friends. To pay my bills, to keep this roof over my head and bread on my table. If it weren't for this double bind of a place I'd be sleeping underneath an archway somewhere drinking meths and lighting fires to keep warm. This place...? It was like this...

Eventually the booze got the better of him, took long enough I can tell you. Long enough that is for him to gamble away everything we possessed – even the bloody shirt off my back. His liver, kidneys and lungs finally packed up and there he is on a respirator in the hospital and there I am at his side while the bailiffs go into 'our' house (and that's a laugh) and take every damned thing, even the walls, which – along with the kitchen sink – were sold off to pay that bas…, sorry but you can see why I can't keep a civil tongue in my head… to pay that man's debts. I sat by his bedside swearing that if he dared to survive, he'd work to pay back every bean to me and then I'd kill him. I wanted him to survive: don't get the wrong idea, true love did not overcome all evils, I wanted him to survive so that I could pay him back farthing for farthing for all that he had made me suffer, made me lose. That much he owed me, the chance for dignified justice. Afraid of prison? Not me, no, I'd be quite happy there, protected, fed, homed and cared about to some degree, cared about more than he ever… But no, you're right, crafty bastard did manage to wriggle out of it… No, no miraculous revival, apology, signing of the pledge and we live together poor but honest: he went and up and died, he did.

On that day, in the hospital when he took his last gasp, I wasn't sure whether to dance on his corpse or shake him back into life. No point to neither anyway, he'd gone, escaped his responsibilities as per. Anyway, Nurse says something like, 'Sorry for your loss, would you like us to advise on the formalities?' Something like that anyway, I turned to her and I said, 'Formalities? Formalities is for you my dear, I don't give a tinker's cuss about him. Chuck him in a ditch as far as I'm concerned.' And with that, I walked out, and no, I don't know, and I don't care what happened next…

I get all sorts here, lots of women – not in the first flush of youth – and they mostly turn out to be widows: widows tend to hunt in pairs. Last week there was this couple: one fat and round like a figure eight and the other thin and tall like something you'd clean a pipe with. Tall one extends a hand to me and says how good it is of me to have them, Doreen – that's figure eight – Doreen has lost her husband last month and she needs… Usual explanation and my face stays all solemn as I listen but inside I'm thinking 'Lost? Well if he was that special why didn't you go out and find him? Careless I call that': meanwhile I'm listening to Eric & Ernie tell me the sad tale and both of them weep all over each other, clutch my hand and say 'You're very good' before disappearing up the stairs to their room. **THEIR** room you notice because once they've handed over their folding money (cash only thank you) it belongs to them for the duration and they can do what they like, or at least most of them think they can which is one of my greatest bugbears...

    ...A few days after I walked out of that hospital, I went back to our place, which was not our place anymore, and let myself in. Almost nothing there except for a cardboard box with a few bits of my clothing, nothing fit for much more than the ragbag. I was surprised the locks had not been changed, I suppose it was early days. And the other thing that was there was a letter from a solicitor. Please, the letter said, would I contact him regarding the will of my late Aunt Susan. Now Aunt Susan was the sister of my mother – I won't use the word 'late' – she was always on time for everything, I'll just say dead which is far more honest. Mother and Susan were the last in the line of their family – strictly speaking I'm the last in the line – Mother never bothered with a husband and as a result my maiden aunt, never spoke to her again after I was born – she pointed a finger at my mother at the time and spoke the dreadful words 'out of wedlock' – I'm glad that sort of attitude has gone out of fashion these days, anything goes which is much nicer. Aunt Susan moved up to this place and as far as I know Mother never heard from her again. So to find this letter was a bit of a surprise but nonetheless, I thought it might be worth pursuing. I went down to the café where I work, 'sorry-for-your-lossing' they were the whole blooming time, but I kept my poker face (ironic that was one thing his gambling taught me – that and teaching me never to gamble) and said nothing. I asked for a few days to myself and they were all too pleased to agree. 'You go away' they said, 'Go away – take

as much time as you need, come back when you are ready.'
So I did...

...They come here with all their bags and traps and
have a 'lovely, lovely 'time and then they go away again
and tell their friends who also come here and have a
'lovely, lovely' time and all the time and I feed my bank
account: after I've taken costs out, it's there, secure and
ready. Mind you, what I have to put up with to get it...

So few of them have any kind of table manners.
There was this one woman – typical really of many of the
sorts I get in here – there she was at the breakfast table, an
accent that was all-fur-coat-and-no-knickers. Her mouth
so full of my farmhouse breakfast she could hardly chew.
'Nmhum, ner, her, neenum' she says, pointing at one of the
paintings. I smile and look puzzled even though I know
what it was she was saying, she parks the food in her
cheeks like some pouchy hamster and, spitting and
spluttering, repeats 'Are these yours?' by which she means
did I paint the cosy, country water colour scenes on the
wall. I smile and nod benignly: she turns to her husband,
spraying chewed food like a bad rain storm and informs
him that they 'simply must have one', and I smile, another
benign one every bit as good as the Pope's, and walk away
taking the dirty dishes with me. When she said 'must' a
gobbet of bacon landed on her husbands specs – the
strange thing being that he didn't even notice: perhaps he
is so used to being showered with her partially digested
food he's grown immune? If I were married to her, I'd
erect windscreen wipers on the food table and sit as far
away as possible.

Anyway, I get the letter, get my wages owed and
toddle off up to the North West where I find that Aunt
Susan has left everything to me, wholly and solely. Which
after everything owing is paid off means that I get this
cottage and a few hundred quid. The best part of it being
that my dear departed left 5 minutes before she did and
the creditors can't touch it. Thank you Aunt Susan, I never
met you but you've done me proud. Me, the last sole

survivor of this inglorious family and when I fade into insignificance without issue then that really will be that. I had no idea, none at all that this bit of luck would befall me. My first reaction is to tell the solicitor to sell the whole kit and caboodle: he shakes his head wisely and says he wouldn't advise it. Nothing sells in this part of the world, the cottage is so isolated no one would want to live there. But Aunt Susan did, I reason, and he says well she was one in a million, actually one in a hundred million and I'd best actually go and see the place before I make a decision because frankly, it would make a good B&B business but wouldn't sell for diddly-squat in its present condition. Ah, I say and nod. He could, he says, make me an offer to take the place of my hands? It's at this point that I realise Mr Solicitor is also a poker player. I nod again, take the keys from his desk and go off to take a look at Aunt Susan's pile of stones...

...Oh they say when they see my scullery, you've still got the fire clay sink, and look (Fred, Syd, Gerald or whatever the name of the day is) look, she still pumps the water into the sink... and the copper... They go into raptures about my beautiful old kitchen with its scrubbed pine table, washing copper and earth floor. We love living so close to nature they say over their muesli. It's homemade or rather home combined since I don't actually grow the oats, raisins and nuts. I do keep hens but draw the line at keeping a pig, they smell no matter what anyone says and the thought of feeding a living creature up for the purpose of eating it revolts me: besides, I get a good supply of bacon and sausages from Wilf down the road who has gone in for this organic malarkey in a big way. Oh, they say, when they see the two-seater privy out the back with its pitcher of washing water and white towel, oh how utterly quaint, so very, very environmental. And strangest of all to me, they choose to use it...

The pile of stones turned out to be an isolated cottage which had not been updated for over a hundred years. I keep the scullery as was because it works as does the very basic kitchen. I can rustle up a decent breakfast for my guests and keeping the copper supplied with fuel is free as along with the cottage came a patch of woodland which provides me with a ready supply of logs. It had four bedrooms, a large loft, two reception rooms and no mains drains or water. Aunt Susan had moved in 50 years previously and got on with life – which must have been pretty hard. Wilf went to take her milk one day and found her on the floor in the scullery, he took her to hospital in his Land Rover but she died, all on her own between clean white sheets and with the smell of antiseptic in her nostrils. She left her body to science and her worldly goods to me and most importantly for the sake of my inheritance, the time of death was indisputably recorded. Very satisfactory I think…

'They' can't help asking if the house is my family home. Family home? Don't make me laugh, it's hardly an ancestral pile. I always smile and say no, I moved in ten years ago and made the place liveable. And that's true, after a few extras in the way of sanitation and piped water, I made the cottage clean, kept it simple and advertised it as a rural retreat for the nurturing of the spirit. For some reason, they like that line you are, they say, a natural healer. I think they believe this because I say so little, I listen as they drone on: 'you see, it was like this, after my relationship broke up I decided that the only thing for me to do was to become a therapist. I have the gift you know, I can empathise and when I do *(slug reading, black hole alignment, happy hippo mud baths or nettle rash release – choose the latest popular concept in money making)* I know I am tuned into the rhythm of the universe. Oh yes,' she/he smiles, 'it's all about simplicity and the cleansing of the inner person. I live simply now'. And yes they do live simply when they come to my B&B; little option really as there is no electricity, the place is lit by oil lamps and candles and I don't have a telly. But then I look outside on the parking space and see the vehicle in which they arrive: generally about as far from nature as Mars is from earth.

The best guests are the ones who come and go leaving no trace of their visit; especially not streaks of excrement down the inside of the toilet pan. They eat their breakfasts quietly, ask no questions and the bedroom always looks as if they never slept in it. I like them, they pay for a night or twos sleep, a little food: they neither expect nor do they give anything more or anything less. The worst kind are the ones who find me by accident. What's happened to them is usually that they have got lost along the way somewhere, get tired and want to book into the first place they can find – sadly it happens to be me. Thirty quid's thirty quid so I can always find them a bed, I do wonder if it's worth it though. Initially they're everso grateful but when they find out they will be living the simple life… 'I can't find the socket for my hair tongs, phone, ibook, camera or what have you' their faces crumple up in disbelief. I explain what I already have explained about the electric and they look at me in irritation. Why is it that modern humans are unable to survive without their vast array of gadgets? It's my opinion that this will be the human doom, the last great power cut and we'll be extinct. It hardly matters to me, I think the planet will be glad to be shot of us in the long run…

…Goodness me, is that the time? It's been nice talking but really must get on I've a party of four Buddhists arriving at six this evening and I haven't made up their beds yet. They have asked if they can meditate in the garden, as long as they cough up the readies, I don't mind what they do. …No, you're right, there are some things I draw the line at, gambling being the obvious one, but on the whole, I live and let live…

…Now remember, stick to the straight path through the woods until you get to the corner, then hop over the broken stile…cows? No, Wilf prefers his pigs… you'll be fine. Lonely, me? Never, you can be alone without being lonely, I've got my hens, my painting and all those bloody sheep…"

20.Bread

The dusty flour rises on the air as she sifts it into the stainless steel mixing bowl, it is followed by grains of dried yeast, sugar, salt and sunflower seeds. Yeast is a living organism. What do living organisms need if they are to flourish? Water, warmth and food – the water will come soon, it will be warm to the touch but not too warm as this would kill the yeast. The sunflower seeds hit the sides of the bowl on the way in, they make a sound like rain on glass, their purpose is to add texture, to give the bread a bit of extra crunch. It's a mixture of flours she has used: a little barley, a little white cake flour (she'd no bread flour in the cupboard and the shops were closed) and khorasan. The latter makes up the bulk of the flours and she chose to buy it because it sounded romantic. The navy blue paper packet told a story: 'Kamut grain is a khorasan wheat, titicum turgidum. Said to be the wheat of the Pharaohs, the crop produces bold golden ears of striking long black awns or whiskers'. This grain was the grain the Pharaohs ate, it was used to make their bread, probably buried alongside them in those great pyramids to feed them in the afterlife.

She wonders, is this the grain that Joseph so carefully stored up against famine? Is this the grain that shared a sack with a silver cup? Long, black whiskers, the grain, she thinks sounds like a pussy cat – but then the Egyptians liked cats. Titicum turgidum – so the internet tells her – has two grains per spiklet, another of nature's lessons in symmetry and in Latin too. She, of course, never learned Latin, sec.mods never taught that sort of thing, it wouldn't be much use to the proles they were expected to turn out. She likes the word 'spiklet', wonders if should read 'spikelet' but can't be bothered to check: it's not important. In the sunshine, her dog has 'bold golden ears', so he has something in common with the bread she is baking.

Until fairly recently, she would have insisted on making the bread by hand. This is the way she was taught. Put the ingredients with the correctly measured warm water into a large bowl, put your hand into the bowl and use it to combine. At first, when she put her hand into this pasty mess, it felt gluey, impossible; but as she beat against the sides of the bowl the dough began to form, initially sticky but with rhythmic, strong beating it would clean the sides of the bowl and form a large ball. The dough would then be turned out onto the floured, wooden table top and kneaded for five minutes. The dough would be warm beneath her fingers, malleable to her bashing right hand fist and turning under the movement of her left hand fingers. To make bread is to link hands down the generations to the beginning of time when the first humans began to experiment with fire and grain.

Now she makes the bread in her Kenwood using the wonderful dough hook – an artefact straight out of Peter Pan. The mixer motor rumbles and whirs as slowly, she adds the water and the oil, slap, beat, whir, slap beat whir. She's grateful now for this mechanical help, she no longer has the strength in her arms and hands to knead with any kind of energy, slap, beat, whir and the dough cleans the side of the bowl, creeps up the hook and has to be pushed back down again.

She puts the dough to prove over a basin of hot water, makes herself a coffee and sits to allow the first rising. This will take ninety minutes. She sips and looks at the dog, slumped casually across his bed. He hears a sound and moves to look out of the window, two paws resting on the crosspiece, nose pressed against the glass. He wonders whether to bark, he watches, his tail quivers a little but he remains a silent watcher. He jumps down, hovers undecided between bed and chair, finally returns to his bed, making a trampling circuit before he finally settles down.

The coffee is good, Fair Trade so no pangs of conscience but full octane, so the delight of something not strictly allowable, not exactly good for her. The family, when she was a child, drank Camp Coffee, a sweet, syrupy liquid, a combination of coffee essence, sugar and chicory. It was mixed with warm milk, more sugar was added: this was coffee then. Now a bottle resides in her baking cupboard, it's used to flavour coffee cakes, she would never dream of drinking it: far too sweet. The coffee she drinks now is brewed from ground Arabica beans. One memory tumbles into another as she waits for the bread to rise. Her mother did not bake bread for the family, the bread was delivered to the house every day and it was always warm.

The sun always shone when she was small it must have rained sometimes but she could not recall it. In the Marley tiled hallway stood a 30s table with barley twist legs and two drawers. It was stained a tarry brown, it smelled of old wood and polish: it lived just inside the front door. Now, in those halcyon days, front doors were never locked – what would be the point? The baker owned a Morris Minor van, it was dark green and inside it had wooden shelves for the bread. When the van stopped outside the house she could just see the top of it over the privet hedge. The baker would open the van doors, take out the family loaf and place it on the hall table. Now, the trick was to be in the right place at the right time. The right place would be half way down the stairs, the right time would coincide with the arrival of the bread, the front door would open a little way, a hand would appear and the bread would be placed. On truly sunny days, she would be exactly where she would need to be, reach the loaf down and sit on the bottom stair. What bliss to recall the nibbling of the crust, the warm loaf resting in her small hands. Her mother never told her off about this, never commented on the lack of hygiene, never reduced her share of the bread – doorstep slices, always thickly spread with butter from New Zealand.

She drained the coffee, checked the rising dough and left the kitchen. She whistled for the dog, called his name, time for a walk, the dough would work its magic without her help, the kitchen was warm, sunshine was pouring in. Left to itself the dough works: Yeast creates carbon dioxide which stretches the structure of the flour and forms millions of tiny air bubbles. The saddest part about the yeast is that in order for the bread to be edible, the yeast has to die.

When she returns from the walk, the dog shakes himself, laps water noisily and settles once more in his bed. On the far wall of the kitchen there is a pine dresser complete with shabby, patterned oddments of china, a long oaken table and a rocking chair, and, of course, the dog curled up in his bed. This kitchen is the hub of the house, no matter how many rooms, or comfortable spaces, this is the place where everyone gathers, where they are most likely to linger, to talk, to simply sit, listen to nothing in particular.

She returns the bowl to the Kenwood and gives it a second kneading: a second jumbling where the dough is knocked back, the air - which the yeast has so carefully troubled itself to breath out – is knocked back, knocked out and the risen dough is reduced in size. This time the dough is formed into the shape or style required after baking: a loaf, rolls, a plait, a tin, a bloomer. Some of these names may have meaning for you, some no meaning at all: it is one of joys of this small union of even smaller counties that the names for the different shapes and sizes of bread can vary, not just from country to country but from county to county. It is remarkable to think that a bread you call a 'bap' in one county can become a 'teacake' only a few yards across the boundary to the next county. It's a secret code, a new language you must learn if you as an 'off-comer' are to make headway in a new community.

Today she is making a simple loaf, a tin shaped loaf. After the second proving and before she places the dough in the oven, she will make two deep diagonal cuts with a sharp knife. She'd like to think this has some profound significance but it doesn't; it just makes the finished bread look nice. Knocked back and placed in a well-oiled baking tin, the dough is now ready for its second and final proving. This time she places it on the cooker top and covers the dough with a warm, wet tea-towel to stop it drying out. She turns the oven on so that it will heat to maximum, the rising warmth will help the bread its second rising. She sings to herself as she wipes down the Kenwood, washes up the bowl and the dough hook. Some of the flour has spilled onto the worktop, she takes a damp cloth and brushes this into her hand, she empties the mess into the black kitchen bin, it's lined with newspaper. The second proving will take 40 minutes, there is no point trying to hurry the process: the washing machine has completed its cycle, she empties it. The dog follows her out into the garden where Spring is showing off its most vibrant display of colours. The apple tree is covered with drifted pink buds, crocuses peep in the borders, the grass smells green, glows green, is green. The washing line is strung between two trees – the apple tree and a silver birch. She knows that some day, someday sooner than she'd like to contemplate, the birch will have to be cut down, it's getting old, parts of it are rotten, a heavy wind will fell it. Much more sensible she knows to organise this, to not leave it to chance but she cannot bear to be the one who decrees a death sentence on this tree, on any tree. It feels too much like sacrilege: maybe in the autumn? Maybe next year sometime? Maybe they'll move and she won't have to make the decision? She pegs the wet towels on the line, a light breeze makes them flap lazily, wafting the soapy scenty smell of washing powder across the garden, it competes with that of the apple blossom and a pale narcissus which peeps up from the bole of the apple tree.

Returning to the kitchen, she places the wicker washing basket back on its hook behind the back door. She whistles for the dog to come in but he is happy enough sniffing and peeing in the four corners of the garden: leave him, she thinks, he'll come when he is ready. Whistling tunelessly she peels the damp tea-towel away from the risen dough, opens the oven and places the tin within its hot, dry belly. She thinks a quiet requiem for the yeast which will die within the first few minutes of baking. Initially, the first blast of heat will cause the yeast to puff the dough up higher than ever, this dying shout of glee will be its valediction, its memorial etched into the crust of a loaf. Greater love hath no yeast: bread of heaven, bread the staff of life, bread, dough, bread and butter. Her train of thought is broken by a gentle thump, thumping on the timber frame of the back door: the dog has finished exchanging 'pee-mail' with other creatures and wants in. She opens the door for him and as she does so notices an edge to the breeze, a spring chill which serves to remind her that it is not summer – cast not a clout it seems to chime as she closes the door. The dog rubs his face up against her legs, an affectionate, lazy rub: she caresses his ears and murmurs sweet nothings to him about his beauty and sheer loveliness. Dogs don't purr, though somehow this one seems to manage something which is a cross between a growl and a sigh of contentment. She turns down the heat of the oven, the crust is formed, the yeast is no more and the dough must cook more slowly now. She wonders about more coffee but notices a slight trembling in her hands which makes her think that it will not be such a good idea.

So she sits, she rocks, she strokes the dog. An observer, if there was such a one to witness her sloth, might think these final twenty minutes wasted: she is simply sitting, rocking, stroking. Her eyes are unfocused, she is not looking out of them: her breath is shallow, her face relaxed. This is not sloth, the observer is a fool, this is being, appreciating the beating heart, the flowing blood, the expanding lungs. Twenty minutes being a being. It is luxury, it is essential it is the experience of nothingness which leads to a knowledge of everything.

Time 's up. The loaf is baked. The aroma wafts memories through the kitchen and into the farther reaches of the house. The bread is out of its tin; it is resting on a cooling rack: glows golden in the spring sunlight.

21. Returning Back (Part 1) CE:2167
Chapter 1 – Muriel

My name is Muriel Apodidomi, I'm 97 years of age and I've always dwelt in this house: my family bought it in the year 2007. I was the only child of only children, never could see the point of marriage – or children for that matter - thus I'm the last in a long line of a family which dates back to something the historians seem to get quite excited about called the Doomsday Book. Recently my friend, Doris Haber popped round to see me: her visit left me thinking.

"Well, said Doris as she glanced round my kitchen, "you certainly keep this place in apple pie order. Those PIKEA chairs are worth a fortune now the Millennium Retro Look is coming into fashion. I heard Fanny Q'Ndm say that a pair like those went for 300 the other day. ..and as for that dresser..."

"Parana pine, Doris, made by my great-great-grandfather – I've told you that on more than one occasion. And before you say any more, the coffee cups were collected by his wife – she seemed to go in for that sort of thing." I commented.

"She had an eye for it then, a great investment for the future, Mu. ...And you've kept it all so lovely, real tribute to your mother. I've only ever been able to imagine what the rest of the house must be like.." hinted Doris.

Doris was being nosey as usual but I never let anyone go beyond my kitchen and downstairs loo. I wax polish the kitchen floor and the dresser once a month. Wash down the contents of the dresser every Tuesday and wash and clean other cupboard contents on a Friday. The lavatory is cleaned thoroughly every day and a clean hand towel awaits any visitor – not that many come but when they do they comment on my 'old world' hospitality and ask wherever I manage to find the tablet of sandalwood soap. As Doris often observes, 'everything gleams' with ...with what though?

All of them hope to be invited upstairs, the house is on three floors, but I never permit that. "I do love that frock you're wearing Doris dear," I smiled gently to change the subject. "It looks so cool..."

Doris bounded in with an excited response, "It's pure cotton muslin and the little sprigs of yellow flowers were based on a Magenta Phiri design – I could never afford the real thing of course but something as pretty this now that fabrics are off ration, well." And Doris smiled at me contentedly. The ration books finally went last year: ten years now and the peace still holds.

"I must say after all these years digging for victory, I think we deserve some kinds of little treats don't you?" she asked sipping the cup of real, fresh bean coffee I had made for her. The coffee, real coffee I mean, is the one thing I've indulged in since rationing went out. Twenty years of war followed by ten years of austerity and now in this last year the brakes are finally, tentatively being taken off.

"Do you remember, Mu, the day war broke out? I still shake when I think of it -World War Three – I was terrified."

"I can't think of anyone who wasn't. All that stuff about shelters and potato sacks, tins of beans and gas masks. No one seemed sure." I mused.

"No one at all... all those government warnings about what to do and when. Strange wasn't it?" Doris helped herself to more coffee, slyly adding two lumps of sugar as though she thought I wouldn't notice.

Let her, I thought, it doesn't matter, "It was strange Doris love, very strange. We'd prepared for the worst - I shared a shelter with the Patel–Mundies - I felt so sorry for them with their little family. Shahia was only 3 months old and Dareth was just coming up for two years."

"I know – I went down to my son and his partner and the grands – the parents were on standby for call-up. It seemed cruel to me to split families up at that point."

We both sat holding hands in my family kitchen, at my family table in my family home all of which had survived intact where so many other things had not. We looked into each other's eyes, noted the tears and laughed. "Silly old fools," we said simultaneously.

It hadn't seemed like it at the time. Shooed into shelters by an army of bossy, scared wardens as the sirens went off across the country. Then sitting there waiting, three days of silence and waiting, waiting. We tried not to speculate, tried not to imagine. I was lucky of course, I only had myself – but the Patel-Mundies and countless people like them with family scattered across the globe?

"I still can't get over it though, all those years..."

"Yes," I sighed "...all those years. The protest marches, the threats, the ban the bombers, the peaceniks, the debates..."

"...the we will if you do..." chimed in Doris.

"...and then the realisation." I smiled. The realisation that for two hundred years the world had been held in the thrall of a bluff; a bluff so big that it passed from generation to generation unquestioned. The problem was that once realisation dawned, and the 'phoney war' was over the real war began.

"I found it really hard you know," Doris told me, "I thought that in all the years of mixed up muddled human soup nothing like that could happen."

"You're right Doris, I think we all felt that way. For me it was pretty straight forward, I'd always known that we were in the 'Book', it was a fact but of no great interest, not even when I realised that I will, as it were, be the final word in our particular chapter once I pop off."

"You pop off?" Doris laughed loudly, "You lass are as fit as any flea that bit the backside of a dairy cow! I reckon you'll surprise us all by marrying late and giving birth to twins on your hundredth birthday."

I can think of nothing I desire less, the thought of being with Some One after all my years of independence revolts me. Oh, I know Doris meant kindly and I laughed along with her but all the same…

And that set me thinking. How would I dispose of my property, what on earth should happen to it? You see, my life has been one long episode of make do and mend, jam tomorrow, pie in the sky when you die: all sayings I learned from my first consciousness. At 97, though I've shrunk to four feet eight inches in height, I am, as Doris so colourfully points out, in pretty good shape. As an infant I survived all of the statutory infantile diseases: passed each one with colours leaping off the mast: I've still got my record card full of the regulation vaccines. I remember that horrible soya milk mother made me drink, I hated it even when Mum let me choose the colour of my straw: obedient child that I was I never thought of refusing it.

I was trained as a cleaner by my mother and to be honest, I've cleaned my way through life. I think I can say without boasting, that I was always valued by my employers for being discreet, silent and reliable. When I finally retired from cleaning on my 90th birthday, I used the time to deep clean my entire home.

"Doris," I said startling us both out of our private reveries.

"Oh! You nearly caused my heart to stop." She laughed, "I was just thinking about that blue cup of yours, up on the right hand side of the dresser, you know, just by the opaque orange one, it must be worth…"

I cut her short, "Hundreds. Yes Doris, I know that, I'm aware that this house is a museum of living history and that I quite casually use pots that have been around for centuries without a thought for what they might be worth. But Doris, what does it all mean?"

"Mean?" Doris looked at me blankly and then thought, "It means, Mu, that your family has built up a wonderful treasury of the past. So many things have come into this place and so few ever gone out. I've only ever seen this bit but if this is anything to go by..." This was more than the usual heavy, ever hopeful hint.

"Doris," I said firmly, "Whatever you may have heard or believe or been told by your mother, you can have no idea. None at all." I was surprised by the bitterness in my own voice.

You see, as I deep cleaned, delving into the random accumulations of each floor, bundling up, tying up, cataloging: I began to wonder why? This house is now 167 years old, my ancestors bought it brand spanking new. It was constructed of sturdy red bricks and concrete blocks, insulated to the prevailing standards of the time and though tatty round the edges, it's in good shape considering its venerable age and the fact that it's survived violent and prolonged action. My dear friend Doris is right when she says it's a treasury of the past, and truth be told, not a dead past but a past living in the present – I've shunned most of the modern gadgetry. I've found it preferable to use things that are familiar to me, notions that my own mother, and father too, taught me. Oh I am well aware of the things people whisper behind their hands, they glance up at the place as they pass, hoping for something though I'm not sure what. And actually, if they really knew what's here, they would probably slap a preservation order on it straight away and claim it as 'heritage', therefore, not mine to dispose of.

I heard Doris's voice through a haze of emotion: she seemed to be making an inventory. Our family home is furnished in a ragbag of styles dating from Victorian times onward. The Parana Pine dresser, the PIKEA-Poang leather and birch chairs. The oval dining table at which we now sat was inherited from a maiden aunt sometime back in the 1970s. It was brought into the house with the intention of replacing it with something more modern when the money was there...the coffee cups, the nick-nacks, the pots, pans and china. It's all there, a living history and rare only in so far as it has survived the ages. There are no carpets – I remember those wooly, patterned terrors that always seemed to me to smell of wet dog – I've never bothered to replace them. It seems so odd now, looking back, the things we were required to do in the national interest – surrendering our carpets being one of them. What on earth was that in aid of? The tacks remain, as do some rather vicious strips of wood studded with sharp pins in the thresholds and on the stair risers: it's as though they could conjure up the idea of a carpet where no carpet is. I suppose I should get them removed.

"...and that veg steamer – Inhabitit that came from and built to last." Doris concluded her totting up. "Why if you put the whole lot up for auction you'd make a mint of money – you could tour the world... you wouldn't need to go alone," she smiled. "I'd come with you and we'd p'raps pick up a couple of bonne jeune hommes." Doris laughed merrily at her old joke.

I laughed too. One of the things I love about Doris is that there's no side on her. She's a good pal and I've known her long enough for us to be able to share moth eaten jokes and complete the end of sentences so often repeated between us that really they don't need to be spoken. We're different people with different backgrounds – the thing we share is a birth year and at our ages, this is one hell of a privilege; neither of us takes it for granted.

Suddenly my own mood changed, I felt solemn, sad, "Doris if it hadn't been for that bloody Profligator, none of this need ever have happened. We'd have discovered the bluff, made friends with the 'others' and the comparative years of peace begun in 1945 would have continued. Instead what? Twenty odd years of pointless conflict."

"I remember the shock when it turned into a conventional sort of bows and arrows type war. All that dynamite..."

"...all those blown up buildings, all those sunken vessels carrying food supplies. And us of course, the usual casualties of war." Neither of us was bitter, just dumbfounded: we'd been caught up in a conflict which was not of our making.

Doris grinned, "Never mind that Profligator – I reckon rationing was the biggest blow! I couldn't get a Gypsy Cream for love nor money for the whole duration – even now I can't afford to buy 'em – who'd have thought Ninety-Two and a half for a packet of 12? It's more than my pension!"

"Rationing didn't upset everyone Doris, the dieticians thought this was a jolly good thing: morbid obesity eradicated at a stroke." I reminded her.

"Well I still say, as my old mother did before me, a little of what you fancy..." she licked her lips. "Have you seen the new style fairy-cakes ? They are so big you can hardly get your mouth round them. Lots of the old stuff is coming back in."

"I'm not so sure it's a good thing," I replied. "Did you see that broadcast from the Global Government the other day: 'Make Cake not War'?"

"I did," said Doris very decidedly, "and I have to say I rather liked it."

"Careful Doris – I've been reading some of the articles about it and there is a lack of consensus . Some folks are saying that cake rather than money is the root of all evil. Have you heard about that new book The Victorious Sponge: Cake or Apocalypse?"

"Victoria sponge be buggered," Doris banged the table, "Shadow DNA testing caused it. All people had to do was to post a smidgeon of their shadow into the Bosun/Higgs Profligator – they'd hardly notice it had gone provided they stayed out of full sun – and hey-presto, their entire DNA history could be mapped, in detail down to the shirt buttons of the most distant ancestor."

"I have to agree with you Doris - suddenly, human beings whose procreation had been muddled up in the melting pot of mixed marriages, sperm donation, egg donation and all that jazz, became dissatisfied with their lot. They felt that, having discovered exactly who they had been, it was up to them to begin reclaiming their heritage."

Doris sniffed, "Heritage my backside. Blooming silly fiction the lot of it – caused twenty years of unnecessary fear and heartache, I'm damned glad the Profligator's been made illegal by the Government."

I am too, but you see, the whole concept of heritage/inheritance remains. The World Government must retain its awareness of the damage all that stuff can cause if it's never allowed to rear its head again.

... And here am I, sitting on what I consider to be a powder keg. And that, after I closed the front door on Doris, is what set me thinking. As I thought, I remembered a young soldier who knocked on my door during the final few weeks of the war.

"Hello there, "he said, "My name's Ban Darkley and I'd be most grateful if you could give me a glass of water, I am very thirsty." He was a curious sight, but then so many of the WWIII warriors were. Ban (short for Banerjee he told me later) had chosen to serve as a Roman Style Centurion .

Chapter 2 – Ban Darkley

"You see Miss Apodidomi," he explained as he slaked his thirst at my tap, again and again and again. "I chose centurion because I have a great admiration for their methods of hand to hand fighting, and Roman because, well, my SDNA shows that I'm descended from the line of Caesar Augusta; it felt right to become one of the Roman Assignants and defend the family honour."

Ban was such a pleasant fellow, not at all threatening. He chatted to me about life, the universe and everything: even asked if he could have a quick 'squizz' at my antique copy of Mrs Beeton. Whilst Ban was talking I noticed his battle dress. It was completely authentic: the leather caliga, pteruges, lorica squmata and animal skin helmet (this he had placed on the kitchen counter whilst he was drinking). The rig was pretty well-worn, the leather boots had definitely seen better days and must have marched thousands of miles, they were almost worn through where the metal studs had fallen out - but there was something missing.

"Ban," I exclaimed, "you have no gladius!"

He gave me a sheepish smile. "It's like this Miss Apodidomi, by the time I joined and became an assignant most people had got rather sick of the bombs, arrows and so on and we were looking for something different. When I signed up I had been studying a book - Less Aggressive Methods of Aggression. I concluded that using drums was the best way: they are loud and noisy – they ratch up the decibels for sure but they don't actually cause any blood to be spilled. Oh," he smiled ruefully, "except mine..." Ban showed her his calloused and broken knuckles. He then spoke about his marches across the globe.

Now I have to say I liked this lad, he'd seen rough times and seemed to have acquired a wisdom well beyond his years. I liked the idea that he'd chosen to be a drummer rather than a fighter - to baffle the opposition into submission rather than blowing off their heads seemed to me a better way. There was a modesty about him which I liked, and an honesty which I felt I could trust. "Ban," I said, tentatively, "it seems that this war will soon be over."

"Yes," he replied, "Fantasiamass at the latest."

"But how will the peace begin? How will it hold? Have you any idea?" I am not sure what I hoped for but if anyone could tell me, I was sure this young man could.

"I predict," he smiled, "that this war will fizzle out. Not one assignant has really got their heart in it. Many more people are using the less aggressive technique – some are actually sitting at tables talking – now that's a new twist!"

"But Ban, how will we keep them talking?" I liked his optimism but I needed more.

"Global government, a single rule of law for the whole world – the Golden Rule common to all peoples: Do unto others as you wish to be done to."

"As simple as that?" I smiled thoughtfully.

"As simple as that and with the additional understanding that all property is theft..." suddenly he broke off speaking and replaced his animal skin helmet. "So sorry Miss Apodidomi, I must go. I'm due for a spell of look-out duty at the top of Paper Mill Hill... Thanks for the water..."And with that he was gone.

The concept of Global Government has been in place for about eight years now, it seems to be working to a degree, The Golden Rule seems to be helping – that and a combination of the 'Hands-off' approach being adopted world wide. But his final idea – all property is theft? I had hoped he would come back and talk some more but I never saw him again.

As I say, Doris's visit, disturbed me, I was aware of an avaricious gleam in her eye that I had never seen before. I began to wonder how long it would be before she asked for a 'small something', you know, just to mark our friendship. She does have a large family, this stuff could benefit them – but it would also weigh them down. All property is theft, Ban told me, as the years have passed I think I begin to see what that really means.

The thing that troubled me more was the concept of how to get rid of my inheritance. All of the people I might like to have willed it to are either dead or almost dead. I have no 'nice young friends' who might benefit. I admit that I retain respectful memories of Ban Darkley - he's done very well, Professor Ban Darkley now. I admire him but to make him my legatee based on a 20 minute conversation eleven years ago seems a false logic. Besides he's a wealthy man now, what with his war memoirs, his novels - many of which are snapped up for screen plays and his Professorship in Early Roman history. What need has he to be burdened with my possessions?

A few days after Doris's visit, I took a different route for my constitutional. Usually I pass up through the town and towards the bowling green – it's looking a sight more healthy than it did even a couple of years ago. The green keeper really knows her stuff. No, this time I decided to skirt Paper Mill Hill and walk along the winding river bank.

I looked up towards the summit where, a few years back, I had last seen Ban as he strode up and down monitoring activity on the Firth – at that stage the most likely threat to us came from the Reivers who dominated the border lands. The morning sun glanced off the hill now, reflecting on the waters of the sweet flowing River Nellen. Around me gleams of light cast halos on all things created, a thrush sang loudly, a dunnock whistled an accompanying recitative. Small things rustled in the undergrowth. Oxeye daisies, bladder campion, ragwort, celandine and buttercups vied with each other in a graceful, glorious dance. Seeds from a dandelion blew above the verdure. I listened and thought that I could hear the whispering song of The Earth. Initially the whispers were difficult to make out, the voice was sweet and low, warm, soft, caressing, but as I walked I tuned in to the rhythms of the Earth's voice. It seemed to be speaking directly to me, "All things come from me, of my own do you give me..." All things, I thought. 'All property is theft,' Ban's words echoed. Then Earth spoke again, "Dust to dust... From me you came, to me you shall return..." The Earth's message and Ban's words seemed to blend into a sort of ad hoc symphony in my head with the birds, insects, flowers, wind and trees as the living orchestra. An age passed, understanding was born. The answer was startlingly simple – little short of everything is required by the Earth and from me.

This made such sense, all property is indeed theft. We (the human race) have assumed too much, taken too much. Although I cannot redress this fault for everyone, I can start to make reparation for my part and the part of my ancestors by returning back all that we have taken.

Chapter 3 – Muriel

I made a list of all that I possessed under three headings: Return To Dust, Return To Flame, Return To Earth. On Midsummer's Day I started digging. Even I was surprised at the energy I generated, certainly not one of my neighbours credited me with the reserves of strength I drew on.

"Here lass, couldn't you do with a hand?" asked young Crellin from two doors down. He's a nice lad, young family and a decent job with the local council.

I refused the offer but kindly, at this stage I really did feel that the task was mine alone. However, at regular intervals Crellin or his partner would appear at the fence with cups of tea, and sometimes sandwiches: always gratefully received. "Here Miss A," Crellin's other half would say, "this'll help to keep you going." They'd sometimes ask me what it was in aid of and when I evaded explaining what I was doing, comforted themselves with the notion that I was preparing a bed for asparagus.

Their little lad came out to see me one of the sunny days, "Misslapodiddle," he said, "are you digging to Stralia?" His question was earnest, hopeful.

I chuckled, I remembered being his age and digging down to the land of Oz with my pal Greta. "No Jevin, not today."

"Maybe tomorrow then?" he lapped his tongue round the mess of a cone he was consuming.

"I think I'd melt like your ice-cream if I tried that," Jevin and I began to laugh in the uninhibited way only the very old can share with the very young: those at ages in between would consider us an embarrassment. Indeed, our hilarity brought Young Crellin out, full of apologies for Jevin being a nuisance. He marched the lad back down their garden not hearing my protests. I would have liked Jevin to stay.

As the days and weeks passed the neighbours realised that I was up for some greater challenge. The hole became a crater so deep that I was obliged to use a ladder to climb down into it. I took all of the internal doors out of the house, dragged them out on a blanket and used them to shore up the walls of my crater. Mr. Vendyvarley of number 29 asked me outright if I thought perhaps there would be a nuclear war after all. Was I building an underground shelter? "Have we, Miss Apodidomi, been lulled into a false sense of security?" His face was all concern, he was old enough to know about M.A.D. (Mutually Assured Destruction) fear remained etched on his brain.

I gave him a reassuring smile and explained "I am returning everything back," and continued digging. Mr. Vendyvarley walked away looking puzzled and not at all reassured.

Now, it's all very well digging a flipping great hole at my age. It was one of the most enjoyable projects I have ever engaged with. The whole time I dug, The Earth seemed to sing, so sweetly, as if encouraging me in my task. As if telling me I had got it right, got it right at last. By the time the crater was a size which I perceived as suitable, it was nearly October and the autumn rains were starting to crank up.

Denny, the daughter of one of my old employers came for a visit. "Hmm," she said as she dipped a bit of butter shortbread into her hot chocolate, "that's quite a feat Mu. But what are you going to do about stopping a flood?"

"I've thought about that," I replied. "Do you think you could give me a hand before you go?" We sat and ate biscuits for a while, I caught up on all her family gossip – who'd hatched, matched or dispatched. Her dad's bid for a place in the Global Government and why he wanted it. And then, we put on rain coats took a tarpaulin, crackly with age but still leak-proof and Denny helped me to peg it down over the hole. "You know Mu," Denny murmured as we fastened the tarpaulin more securely, "I'm not sure this is going to be enough."

"Not enough?" I queried.

"I'm no expert, but I think that rain causes the water table to rise and as it rises your crater will turn into a swimming pool – I am guessing that's not what you were hoping for?" Denny grinned.

"I never did learn to swim Denny and I don't fancy doing so now." I laughed. "But how the heck are we going to avoid it happening?"

We returned to the house and drank more chocolate, Denny rifled through my food cupboard for more shortbread, "You know Mu, I love the way you make shortbread using that thistle form – you're an artist!"

I looked at the mould, it was polished smooth with age though quite what age I had no idea: the form had been around far longer than I had. I traced its curves and thought for a while about my mother's hands, kneading and bashing the paste for the shortbread. Sometimes a strand of her hair would fall across her face as she worked; she'd raise a curved and floury hand to push it back behind her ear. As I thought, it seemed likely to me that my mother in her turn had watched her mother make shortbread. The recipe had never changed, as far as I knew, it had been passed hand to hand down the centuries. I smiled to myself, was there shortbread in the Doomsday Book? The sycamore from which the form was made was a pale, bland, cream worn smooth with time. I raised the form to my face and took a deep sniff at the wooden buttery scent it had developed over time. As with all the things in my care, the form itself must be returned to earth. Should I make a gift of it to Denny? I hesitated staring for what seemed an eternity, havering over the thought, eaten with indecision. Denny would be delighted to receive it, that much was certain. I put the form away.

Chapter 4 – Denny

I watched Mu as she took a deep, deep sniff at the shortbread form and I knew that above everything, I would like to possess it. It was a thing of immense beauty, simple, real. However, I looked at her face and knew that though she hesitated, she would not be deviated – all must be returned to earth. I respected that, her resilience, her refusal, having decided, to go through with it all. The lack of internal doors was proof of her intention. And then it struck me, a way of draining the crater could be achieved: "Muriel, I have an idea…"

Getting into the washing machine was not difficult, a few screws here and there and the cover was off. "Of course," said Mu, "There'll be the issue of keeping myself sweet and clean now the washer is being reprogrammed!" She laughed, then went quiet. "Denny love, what are you doing at present?"

There was a plea in her eyes, "Not a lot, since my folks split, I've been ferrying between the two of them, listening to their respective woes – which are pretty pathetic…"

Muriel interrupted me, "Never dismiss other people's woes, even if they are your parents. Only the individual can explain what really hurts, and different hurts affect different people in different ways."

"Okay," I replied, "I'm a grown up, their split didn't hurt me at all and honestly I wondered why they hung on for so long," Mu's eyebrows were raised in mild disapproval, "…truce Mu! Now, to answer your question, I'm doing nowt at present – I'm drifting for the rest of the winter."

"In that case, drifter, how about drifting my way for a while?" She looked a little timid about this request. I didn't speak, just put my arms around her: there are few people in this life who are truly special and Muriel is one of them. "Now," said Mu, "about this pump."

It was easy enough to track the washing machine pump to its lair, nestled neatly beneath the drum. I admired its simplicity, a piece of technology which had lasted the ages and never really been bettered, slightly larger than a grapefruit, the plastic yellowed with use, the metal still shiny: three wires were attached to it on clips. Muriel peered over my shoulder, blocking the light. I stood up to let her get a closer look. "You know," she smiled, all these years this thing has worked for me and I've never given a thought to its biology. I remember when mum bought it, it was the latest model at the time."

"Solid stuff, Muriel, built to last. Good job too with all those shortages during the war years."

She laughed, "Wasn't much use when the power and the water went off!" We looked through the kitchen window at the two water butts which, in spite of the growing prosperity everyone kept 'just in case.' "We got so used to it all, washing in a tablespoon of water, storing up dry goods and cans."

"I think it's a good habit to keep, if you look at the profligacy of the 20th and 21st centuries there are lessons we must learn. Now, the pump – I need a smaller screw driver please." And almost before I'd finished speaking, she'd placed one in my hand. I bent down to my work again, touched the metal casing of the machine, there was a loud crack as a spark leapt out at me, "What the...?" I yelped.

Muriel rushed to my aid, "Are you hurt Denny?" I felt clammy with shock, then I began to laugh, "Muriel, if we're going to muck about with electrical stuff, we need to remember to turn the power off first."
"Oh my dear, to think," she said as we both reached over to switch off the machine where it was wired into the mains.

After the excitement of removing the pump, we decided a lunch break would be a good move. I used a bit of scrap paper to work out how the pump could be employed most effectively to keep the crater drained. Muriel inspected the sketch, "You're a clever lass Denny," she said admiringly. "I'd never be able to figure out anything like that."

January proved to be the most difficult month. Despite clothing the pump in a mothy old sheepskin rug the temperatures were so far into the minuses that it froze constantly. We considered boiling kettles, looping up an electric blanket or placing a frame tent over the top to cover it but to no avail: the earth had frozen as if from within. February came and went, icicles made daggers in the trees. Under Muriel's supervision, I made up fat balls to hang outside the kitchen window while she crushed up nuts and seeds for the mesh dispenser. We scattered crumbs of bread and watched the daylight open the curtains on each new day and the poor cold creatures came to feed. One morning in early March Muriel sat with me at breakfast and said, "The snowdrops are over, the daffs are starting to show their faces: time for you to be off Denny."

I was shocked, I had grown so used to her ways, become so much part of her life that I had forgotten I would have to move on. She was right. "Denny, to everything there is a season," but to accept these words: final, no turning back…

Muriel was such a steady, quiet person. I'd known her since my earliest childhood, she was part of the fabric of my life. In those few months she wove herself more nearly to me so that when she made the final return, a little of her, was truly part of me.

Chapter Five - Emver Gail

I came onto the scene that April I noticed a card in the post office window. 'Wanted: Young, Strong Helper for heavy duties in return for shelter, food and a small gratuity.' At that time I was kicking my heels, wasn't sure what I really wanted to do anyway. I'd had some odd jobs – cleaning, gardening and so on but it was always difficult to raise the wind to pay the rent. I qualified precisely for the post of helper and the terms looked as though they may well suit. So I applied. I won't say I wasn't startled when I understood what Mu had in mind, anyone would be. The interview took place in an upstairs living room. We sat opposite one another on some flaky old basket chairs – they had definitely seen better days! We were surrounded by neat piles of stuff labeled 'wood', 'textiles', 'paper', 'card', 'other decomposable material'. She explained to me that if I chose to accept the job, my first task would be to break or tear everything in that room into what she called 'bite sized pieces'. "But why?" I asked, "There's some really valuable stuff here." It was then she explained to me about returning back.

"You see," she illuminated, "I have come to understand a fundamental truth:
all property is theft." Proudhon's simple, but highly contentious statement which has been ignored for many generations. What had this to do with this gentle, sprightly old lady? I waited to hear more.

"All of the things I possess at present were either bought, brought, given or inherited," She smiled at me once more, the light in her eyes suggesting she knew I needed more. "However, I repeat, nothing that I possess belongs to me."

"But you say nothing you possess is stolen?" I countered.

"That is correct."

"Therefore you must have title to all that you own. You have no need to feel guilty or wrong in any way." I was concerned, the potential destruction of all her belongings seemed to me – well...

"I'm not mad, Emver," she said gently. "It is true to say that I have title but do I truly possess all of these things? As my life plays itself out, I doubt that I ever owned a thing, I doubt that work earned me the right to possess anything, I doubt that the legacy of others entitled me to own anything."

"Then why destroy it? Why not give it away or sell it?" I was struggling to comprehend.

"Because one of the lessons I have learned, probably the only lesson I have learned, is that to burden others with your past is wrong. Broken down into their component parts, all of these possessions came from the earth - were taken from the earth. From the beginning of time, the earth has been ravaged by human kind for their own selfish purposes. I need to return everything back..."

A couple of days later Muriel showed me to an attic bedroom on the top floor. It had a single bed, bare floorboards and a small chair on which I could put my stuff – not that I had much, the way I'd been living all my stuff fitted into a rucksack. We started work the following day.

"You will share breakfast with me?" Mu had asked the previous evening before I'd turned in: she was always so gracious, never wishing to overstep boundaries. When I went down that morning a feast of home baked bread, boiled eggs and fresh fruit awaited me. I had been living out of take-away bins for a few days as money had got so short, you can imagine just how welcome this was. Mu smiled as she watched me eat, "Food tastes so much better when it's shared, she remarked. "Stoke up, Emver, we've a lot to do today."

We went up to the living room where she provided me with a drill, saws, a claw hammer and screwdrivers of different types: each one was from Locke & Becker – I'd only ever seen photographs of them. Return to earth was our theme at this point. I dismantled, smashed, crashed my way through each neatly ticketed bundle. The paper was easy enough to reduce to reams and tie up, she could handle those: – but some of the really old stuff, kid skin parchment with tiny writing, architects' plans, watercolour pictures, sepia photographs... I need you to understand that I am not a vandal, I appreciate lovely things and to destroy as a deliberate act felt like: hooliganism? an act of willful delinquency? – even now I can't name it. But, having agreed to Muriel's terms and promised to do as she bid, over time I learned to school myself to her way of thinking.

"Muriel," I queried three days in, "these photos.."

"What about them?" she asked resting a small pile of books on a ledge.

"Do you not think... would you not like to, well, to maybe select just a few?"

"What would be the point?" she looked at me quizzically.

"Your past, your family's past..." my voice trailed away.

Muriel peered at me benignly, "These 'people' captured, frozen in time – their time I might add – these people, were, they are not. I have a hazy notion now of how they are linked to me but it no longer matters. I would prefer to return them to the earth, memory Emver, memory is the only thing."

"But when you die, your memory will die with you."

"So much the better, no burden, no footprint only a fading shadow in a few minds"

"You'll be more than a fading shadow to me."

"Thank you, that is a privilege and a comfort. However, should you forget me, nothing will be lost."

By the end of May the earth had warmed and the sun seemed to smile upon us as we threw in the last of the shredded carpet: return to earth was complete. I picked up a shovel to start the process of mounding the crater over with spoil. "Wait," said Muriel. I hesitated, surely not a moment for regret?

Mu went to the shed and brought out two small sacks: "Here she said," I took one, it was filled with a mélange of bulbs, tubers and seeds. She reached into her sack and broadcast the contents across the mouth of the crater; I copied her. "Thank you earth," she smiled as the new life found its place among the litter.

The neighbours, who had by now deduced that Mu was having a 'massive clear out', all helped to fill the crater with the spoil that had come out of it in the first place. It created a low but dainty mound. We mulched the soil with kitchen compost and planted three apple trees, the old varieties. "These," she said as she chatted, "Will be used by the Earth to return something back to you in years to come." It was a statement directed towards all present and clearly gave her pleasure to think of the fruit the trees would bear. "Now," said Mu as she dusted the dirt of her hands "I think it's time for a break. We'll take a week off to plan the next strategy."

Muriel reckoned we needed another head to work out how best to dismantle the house, I had the haziest ideas of how this could be done. I thought for a bit and then suggested a mate of mine who'd recently qualified as an architect. Sherivia was struggling to find work, people remained cautious about the future of the peace.

"What you must be aware of first and foremost is safety. Break the common sense rules and you'll have a problem – I'm assuming you want to live long enough to complete the project?" she asked Mu bluntly.

Mu laughed heartily, "I trust that I shall, I'll do nothing to foreclose on my own life."

"Good," Sherivia said firmly, "if that's the case, you need to get scaffolding put up before you can begin on the rest." For about a ten days, we battled with Sherivia about the whys and wherefores of what we needed to do. She pointed out that if we found any asbestos, everything would grind to a halt until that had been safely disposed of. Then there was the process of deconstruction as a whole. Top down or bottom up? "When this place was built," Sherivia explained, "reinforced concrete girders and panels were used as well as bricks and mortar. If you remove the roof first, how will you shelter yourselves when the weather breaks up? But if you choose to go from the bottom up, you risk destabilizing the whole place and having it tumble round your ears."

We concluded that top down was the most practical way and the old tarp was brought in for duty once more. As the scaffolding went up, the neighbours felt reassured, clearly Muriel was about to have the house 'done up' they told each other: sadly for them, they were soon to be disabused of this notion.

One warm July day Muriel and I, dressed in 'Hi-Vis' jackets, hard hats and safety boots, climbed to the top of the house. "Well?" she looked across at me with a mischievous grin, "you want to go first or shall I?"

"Your house," I stated, "in any case, my mum always taught me that it's lady's first." Muriel raised her claw hammer in the air, pursed her lips and shouted "Geronimo!" as she levered up the first tile, and threw it with considerable force into the empty skip below.

"Shot!" I yelled and levered up the second tile. It may have taken weeks to tile that roof, but we stripped it down in just two days. We had the most immense fun stripping the South West facing slope of the roof: it was almost as though Muriel was competing with me to see who could remove the most tiles.

After 'destruction day one' Mrs. Haber bustled into the house uninvited, "What ever are you thinking of Muriel? Was there an accident? Is that what happened, all your lovely things got destroyed?"

"Sit down and have a cup of tea Doris," Muriel pushed her onto one of the two remaining stools.

"And what's wrong with your roof?" Doris was dumbfounded, dismayed.

I shan't record the conversation here, it's fit that it should be lost to memory. Mrs. B was offended, hurt and concerned for her friend – they had known each other for many years. I'm not sure which hurt her the most, the fact that Mu had returned to the earth the things which had come from it in the first place or the fact that she had done this without so much as a word to Mrs.B. Or was it that Mu had not given her first option on her goods and chattels? The meeting ended in tears, Mu maintained her silence but Mrs. Haber could not resist a few final, angry 'never speak to you again' words. Had the door still been on, it would have been slammed, after Mrs.B left, Mu leaned heavily against my chest and wept into my shirt for the sheer comfort of it.

Chapter Six - Emver Gail

The media started to get interested after we arranged for the scaffolding to be erected. It's a sad reflection to note that despite the general common sense of the world's populace, they still sought thrills, spills and vicarious pleasure through the medium of the gutter press and lurid soaps. The headlines were not flattering:

'MAD MU MURDERS MANSION!'
'all property' theft! swears Sallyport granny'

'It's My House & I'm Giving It Back'
Read all about eccentric Millionaire Spinster - she's giving it all away!'

Muriel was irritated at being called a granny, did not mind the correct but old fashioned term spinster and on the whole, placidly ignored all requests by the press for an 'exclusive'. Thus, with the subtlety of time immemorial, they didn't let the facts stand in the way of a good story.

As with the crater, once the neighbours started to live with Mu's real intentions, they wanted to help her. It's my belief that Borse Q'ndm was the first to ask if she really meant what she had said about returning it all back. Muriel merely nodded in reply; hence, he was the first of many to join in the task and it really helped to speed things up. Children would pile bricks up in stacks, adults would shimmy up and down ladders with hods, many different people brought refreshments – all of this was welcome. I think one of the best days was the day, several weeks after her outburst, Mrs. Haber brought a peace offering in the form of a large seed cake: she handed it to

169

Mu with the words, "Make cake…" and Mu chimed in with the remainder of the sentence before they both dissolved into peals of laughter.

I felt closer to Muriel than I ever did to my own grandmother. Sometimes, when I felt she needed a break, I'd take her home to my mum and she would make small things for Muriel to eat. It seemed to me that Muriel shrank a little more as time passed: she pecked at food like the tiniest of birds.

From August to mid September the sun shone without a break, from the smallest child to the oldest adult, we occupied ourselves with transporting the bricks and mortar – now dust in buckets down to the beach. Some days, the buckets were passed down through family chain gangs, other days, older folks would challenge each other to see who could carry the most, or run the fastest loads. The atmosphere was festive. Some people expressed concern that the beach sand had developed a red glow but a spring tide put paid to those worries as nature showed that she can take care of herself and mixed the whole lot together by the force of the moon.

The end of the summer came abruptly with a massive rain storm, it did not hamper us at all as by that time the entire house had been demolished and its component parts stacked and quantified. The rain, we found was there for the duration, one of the wettest autumns on record which put paid to any further returning back until the following spring. Our shelter having been disposed of, we needed somewhere to stay for a while; I was amazed and touched by the many offers that flew in.

Chapter Seven – Emver & Tomiso

After some discussion we elected to perch with Tomiso Paytel, an old mate of mine. All that was left on the site of Mu's home were the large items - reinforced with steel and iron, the UPVC windows and all the synthetics – these were something of a poser.

We sat one night with Muriel discussing this. "It has to be solved," Muriel smiled at Tomiso, "time is running out." We warmed our hands at Tomiso's open hearth, toasting crumpets on the end of a long iron fork. Silently we munched our way through the crumpets focusing our thoughts on the problem when suddenly Tomiso leapt to his feet:

"This is the answer Mu," he looked excited, "the answer is so simple, you are warming yourself upon it now!"

She looked startled, "Fire Tomiso?"

"Fire!"

"But," Muriel responded, "I knew that this would be the third category all along. The decomposables have been returned to earth, the bricks and so forth have returned to dust. But fire?" I chipped in here to confirm that one of Muriel's stipulations had always been that no further harm should be caused to the earth. "If we burn all of these things, we will pollute the air and the earth, Mu's purpose will be compromised."

Tomiso shook his head, "Uh, uh."

Muriel became quite agitated, "You heard what Emver said, no pollution, so much of this old stuff carries with it the possibility of chemical gases when combusted not to mention the thought of all that smoke."

"The answer is simple –Askja" grinned Tomiso.

"Askja?" repeated Muriel and Emver.

"Askja is a large basaltic volcano - it's in Iceland and it's live. The fire of the volcano is completely natural, Earth will gladly accept and consume the combustibles you have to offer." Tomiso's argument could not be faulted but actually carrying the idea through was another thing. We spent hours researching methods of transport, safe ways of dropping the loads into the volcano and ensuring that our actions would not cause Askja to erupt.

"Could we use the old Land Rover?" I tentatively asked Muriel. "This was one item yet to be dismantled, we had left it until last thinking it might prove useful. It was chunkily sleek, creamy white and of all the things Mu and I had to dispose of, this was the one I truly desired.

"Not only use it but dispose of it as well!" giggled Muriel. Tomiso got there well ahead of me.

The Landy was to be loaded up with all the stuff, an ancient trailer affixed to the back. "But," queried Murel, "it's a heck of a journey – how are you going to get there?" We fetched out the maps and after many hours of discussion figured that the journey would take us around 4-6 weeks by road and ferry and we also needed to consider getting back home – we'd need transport to get to Reykjavik.

"Look," said Muriel, " you are bright enough to work that all out without me – I wish I could come but... well I trust the pair of you to do this bit, I need a bit of 'me' time," she told us. I had noticed that Muriel, though still strong in many ways, had latterly started to slow: her time was coming closer...

Driving the old bus to Askja was both a challenge and a privilege; Tomiso, never one to be shy, had succeeded in getting fuel from his 'connections'. We drove through the landscape used by Neil Armstrong and Buzz Aldrin to train for the first ever moon landing. The final stretch to the edge of the volcano was dramatic. We had managed to research the complex method of engaging the free wheel hubs for the four wheel drive in low gear and found that this was essential for us to navigate our way up the slopes of the volcano. Conversation between us at this point was limited to whoops of joy and groans of fear as we zigzagged, slid, gripped and slid again – the traction with the ashy surface causing a rock and roll of a drive. "Right," Said Tomiso decisively as we arrived at the edge of the Askja, "Now is the time to say goodbye."

I looked at him at that moment, he returned my hard gaze: neither of us wanted to do this, the Landy whom we had affectionately named 'Brenda' for no particular reason, had been a great work horse, so different from the slick Freewheelers of our age: they take away the free will of the operator, no need to think, anticipate or even stay awake once the destination is selected. Brenda had a four manual gearbox, with complex ideas of reverse: for the first time in our lives, we had actually driven a vehicle, been in charge. When I say in charge, it's a relative term as on more than one occasion, Brenda seemed to have a will of her own. "Emver," Tomiso looked at me thoughtfully, "this is one part of the deal where we could cheat a little. Muriel need never know..."

I admit I was so tempted, the minutes drifted by, Brenda poised for her dramatic and final end. "...need never, ever know. You are right Tomiso." And for a while over a cup of coffee on the upper slopes of Askja, we contemplated cheating, where, we wondered, would be the harm? At last, with heavy sighs, we shook hands, hugged each other and moved towards the 'old girl'. "Brenda, we love you dearly," I began.

"And this," continued Tomiso, "is nothing personal. But..."

"...when you gotta go, you gotta go." We finished together, slapping a high five to each other across her bonnet. Now came the hard bit, the part any sane person would advise against. However, we'd seen it done on some old film from the 20th century – Tomiso's particular interest – and thus knew it could be done. Tomiso started up the engine, I handed him two pieces of timber we'd devised for the purpose back in Blighty and he jammed down both clutch and accelerator. The one for the clutch had a piece of rope attached to it. "Count now!" he shouted "**Three, Two One**," I let off the hand brake and yanked on the rope as we both jumped clear through Brenda's doors. She did not hesitate but drove valiantly to her own end at the heart of the volcano: a brief roar then nothing, as she disappeared into its maw.

Chapter 8 ...and at the last.

Tomiso and Emver arrived back in Sallyport at midnight as the clocks were striking and the 21st June began. They found that Muriel lay in a light sleep, Doris and Denny were at her side. "She's been like this for a few days," said Doris quietly. Emver gazed at the old, face, chiseled out by time, lines of worry, lines of laughter, lines of living etched. There was no tension in this face, just a slow letting go.

"What happened?" asked Tomiso, drawing up a chair by Muriel's bedside.

Denny looked up at him, she was holding Mu's hand. "Three days ago, she didn't come down for breakfast, I went to see if she was okay and could not wake her."

"She had been very firm," Doris explained, "about not calling doctors, or meddling in any way," a tear seeped from Doris's eye and trickled down to her chin. "It's very hard on us you know..." her voice faded away, Denny held out her free hand to Doris.

Emver, Tomiso, Denny and Doris were all grouped about the bed, waiting. As dawn broke on summer solstice Muriel opened her eyes, she sought Emver's face, "Remember..." She whispered. He fetched out her remaining possession - a cotton lined wicker basket. With the help of Tomiso, Muriel was lifted into the basket: "Comfortable?" he smiled. They could barely see the nod of her chin. Denny covered Mu with a blanket, Doris kissed her temples

"At last," she whispered, "it is done. Everything this family ever took is returned." She fell into a gentle sleep from which she never woke.

22. Returning Back (Part Two)

(In Conversation with Professor Banerjee Darkley: leading authority on WWIII and its outcomes. This extract is taken from the transcript of an interview with Bubble Sykes dated 08:08:229. B.S.'s commentary on the interview appears in italics)

"...Yes, I remember her very well, even though we only met that once. In time of war for someone to be so open, so trusting. Muriel just let me into her home, gave me what I wanted – a glass of tap water – then sent me on my way with her blessing. She, of course, was hoping like everyone else that the war would be over – 'by Fantasiamass' as we had started to tell each other, only a few of us believed it; the war just seemed to grind on, and on. People had virtually forgotten what they were fighting for.

We stood in her kitchen for a while – it was like being in a time capsule. You can see something like it reproduced in the National Museum *(he chuckles to himself)* not, I think that Muriel Apodidomi would have been amused to see a lasting monument in tribute to her memory!

(His expression changes to a glance of serious sadness) You see, of all the people I ever spoke to at that time, she stands out in my mind as someone who was thinking through the implications of peace, should it ever happen. Her efforts to lead by example were investigated, honoured and accepted: in her memory, the Returning Back Movement began to gather pace. Across the globe, people started to imitate Muriel's actions. Initially, a few hundred brave souls copied her to the letter but as the years went by everyone started to relax into the peace – which may I remind you has now held for over 60 years – consequently the R.B.M. evolved into its present form of symbolic action – did you see the Duchess of Granby crushing that blue china dolphin into small pieces with a

hammer and digging the result into the roots of a rose bush? ...hideous thing, an aberration of good taste in the late 1900s in my opinion, but worth a mint I understand from the newspaper reports. I think from that one meeting with Miss Apodidomi, she would have despised the action and the movement for its shallowness...

Do I think that what she did was right? *(he considers the question in silence for a few minutes)* I'm not sure what the definition of right and wrong is in this case. Muriel did what she felt to be right at the time, at no point did she call for anyone else to imitate: it was right for her... Well yes, you could argue that if individuals only did what felt right for them – say, I don't know...eating babies for example – then we would end up in a chaotic, anarchistic society. But remember this, we live under the structure of Global Government. *(his manner was grave)* if we ever forget it, the peace which has held for so long will end within twenty-four hours. There are no such things as country boundaries, races, religions, colours or creeds: the only law recognised in 2297 is Cause No Harm. The Golden Rule by which all humans must live... *(We sit in silence for a while, contemplating the all-encompassing simplicity of this single law: I shiver, I was born long after the war ended, I have known only the peace of the world.)*

Now, you came to talk to me about the way in which the war ended for me and how I perceived it. You have read 'Actions & Consequences (WWIII On Reflection)' - to be honest all of what you want to know is in there, I wrote 3 volumes after all, carefully researched and based on my own experience... weighty tomes, but they are stuffed with facts and analysis. ...you say you want to meet the real me?

(Professor Darkley places his hands before him in an attitude of prayer. I wait, observing him closely. He's nearly ninety now, his hands are covered with age spots, the calluses from the battle drumming are layered across his knuckles; his wrists, though thin with age, look sturdy and strong. I'm told he still drums for over an hour each day. The

power of the drum, the most ancient of all instruments reaches across the ages to the present day. When all else has ended, the beat of the drum will be heard to earth's dying breath.)

...the real me? *(nodding his head)* I know that Miss Apodidomi described me to her friend as a likeable lad with wisdom beyond my years. Looking back, I think she was probably correct at that time. *(He stops speaking, looks at me intently)* what you must understand is that then I believed I knew everything there was to know. I was confident that I'd found the solution – I was right to be confident as things turned out but whether that was my wisdom or the result of a collective consciousness I can't say...

The me then, dressed in my war torn, battle stained Roman garb. *(He smiles)* It all seemed so important at the time. I think of it as pure good fortune that I read 'Less Aggressive Methods' – you know the book?... Good, it still stands as a model today, though it's veracity has been questioned by some of the more modern historians and political thinkers. *(he pauses)* To think she spotted it... the missing gladius! *(a long pause, I wonder if he has fallen into sleep; with a sudden start his eyes open, as though he is seeing far back into the past. He looks at me for a split second, he had forgotten I was present.)* Ah yes, the eagle eyes of the old, and now I am old myself... I'm glad that old age was not outlawed, I am glad that we are now allowed to reach our allotted time in our own way... for the most part respected and nurtured...

(This conversation is so important to me: I want to get to the real root of things, to the psychology of the ending of the war. Professor Darkley has not only studied and written extensively about WWIII he was there, at the end. He is growing old and tired, he's making his peace with the world before he dies, I want to know what it was all about. What was it like to be part of the anti-climax of all time? The frittered lives? I prompt him).

That day, when I received the gift of water from Muriel, the sun had carried over from the previous day, there was a warm but fresh wind which adjusted the temperature to a pleasant level. As I took up my sentry duty on Paper Mill Hill I breathed the air with a sense of satisfaction, it felt clean. For what seemed like an eternity, the fields, beaches and estuaries of Sallyport had been ravaged by the clash of swords and twang of arrows. Unrest had grown in the ranks of all the different assignants: war had been mis-sold as a 'thrilling adventure' a chance to 'see the world' to 'prove your patriotism'. *(An ironic smile crosses the Professor's face, he looks up at me.)* Had his existence not been soundly disproved, each of the participating factions would have claimed God was on their side. Without God, they had only themselves to blame. "Tears before bedtime" was something Muriel commented to me. It was a few days later that the end began to begin – I joined the raggle-taggle of 'fighters' who drifted to the plains by Sallyport. Can you imagine? A completely mixed bunch of people – folks who had opposed each other in ferocious battles on the previous day now walking, tiredly, arm in arm, talking about the weather…

(As part of my researches I have read contemporary news reports of the day and seen the pictures of a medley of fighting factions: Chinese Warriors, Japanese Samurai, WWI Cavalry Officers, Celtic Fighters offering chariot lifts to tired Pedites, Zulus carrying wounded Goths on hastily constructed stretchers.)

…It makes me laugh to think of what came later - it confounded the Puppet Masters of all nations! *(An edge of anger comes into his voice)* It was their venom and misplaced genetically inherited pride which stoked the original conflict: they had lost their power…the assignants had laid down their slings and arrows in a simultaneous, unplanned world wide act of defiance…

(He breaks off into another reverie. I've made extensive notes from the archives. Initially there were

178

threats of courts marshal, hangings, confiscation of property by the various governments until a sudden collective consciousness dawned upon each one that the Military 'Act of Defiance' as it was initially known was actually an 'Act of Basic Common Sense' What the puffed up world powers began to understand was that their thirst for conflict, confrontation and generally being cross about things was no longer a vote winner. Books like 'Less Aggressive Methods' and other increasingly open secret discussions by the foot soldiers and members of the everso common populace – the silent majority?- encouraged people to think laterally. Lateral thinking caused them to realise that hacking bits off each other wasn't kind, and hacking bits off each other just because you and your predecessors had been doing so on and off for centuries was not a good enough reason to continue. The governments, puppet masters and generals of all factions started talking to each other: by talking they agreed on a form of shared responsibility with which to govern the world. Those first tentative days of peace were so sensible. 'THEY' had read about an ancient but wise principle 'Do as you would be done by' and (excluding certain specific sadomasochistic sects and the like) decided that 'THEY' would adopt a hands-off approach to running the world. But these were things I'd read about, I wanted to know first hand – what did it feel like to be there? Professor, I prompt, softly...)

To be there?... *(a look spreads across his face, animated, awestruck)*...On that last day, something 'other' caused us to gather on Papermill Green: across the world, opposing factions were drawn to similar places as dawn rose. That was the curious thing, the beat began at the same moment across the world – dawn of the same day over a period of twenty-four hours. Our dawn rose over the brow of Papermill Hill: shades of chrome yellow, sugary orange, swirly greys, iridescent blues melted together and coloured the sky. We stood in silence. A beam of light hit the waters of the river, as it did so the lone beat of a Senegalian Jung Jung could be heard. The drummer, his tattered war rags blowing gently in the breeze, struck the drum at the pace of a resting heart beat. We stood in the glow of the rising sun as morning mists burned away and the dew dried on the grass...how long did he beat for? A minute?, an hour?, the whole morning?: I was unaware then as I am now. There came a point for each one of us to take up the beat on the many different drums from the many different cultures represented: I took up my sticks and joined that whispering pulse on my tympanium. To call it music would be wrong because that would convey the idea of a symphony or something consciously orchestrated. It seemed that we heard the earth cry out in pain, as though she was appealing to us to heal her wounds, to cause no further scars. I heard the blowing of a shofar, strange, melancholy; synchronized to the off-beat of the drums and then the drone of a bagpipe which took up a lament. As the day progressed, we were joined on the green, in the streets, upon the hillside by warriors and civilians alike. No one spoke, each one brought some kind of instrument – violins, flutes, ocarina – even I recall, a grand piano wheeled impossibly to the top of Paper Mill Hill. Small children held rattles, triangles: those who had no instrument, beat the rhythm out on saucepans, bin lids and tin cans – anything...

Deafening cacophony? *(again, that pause, that look deep into my eyes as if searching)* No, the beat was the quietest whisper you can imagine, a hush, a lullaby, a lament. We played on through the first twenty-four hours, unceasing, the whole world was held in the thrall of earth's bleeding heart. We played on, on, on, needing nothing but to be part of this. When I look back to that day, I think we were caught up - all caught up - in an act of repentance.

That ancient book of stories which my mother read me as a child told of a man called Noah and a flood. The music of that day brought this story to mind, the concept of a 'god' at the centre of the story who had become angry with a disobedient world, had set out to destroy all that was evil – our flood was a flood of music...

As the twenty-fourth hour passed and a new day started to dawn, the music changed. The melancholy wove into rhythms and melodies of hope – sambas, tangos, mazurkas, rumbas, waltzes, folk tunes. The sounds rose, they were pleasing to the ear, many people put down their instruments and began to dance. Laughter, joy, tears of hope and smiles of discovery spread throughout the crowds, spread across the country, across the surface of the earth. On the forty-eighth hour, the second day of the peace, the colours rose over Paper Mill Hill once more and in the sky, complete, unbroken, was a bow of colour, the music drifted to a whisper and died away on the breeze. Earth had signaled her blessing, we were free to try again..."

Coming in Autumn 2015 –
'The Tragedy Of Charlie Lear'
A novel by Susan Brice

"The room was so fugged it was difficult to see the television screen, the men, contentedly chain smoking and slurping beer from bottles and cans hardly seemed to notice. The subject of the film 'He Stoops To Bonk Her' needs no further clarification and their grunts, groans and lewd comments do not need to be described. That they were in full enjoyment of their faculties was obvious.

Now, you may think this is a party of teenage lads, facial hair mere bum fluff and voices barely broken. Here you would be wrong: the average age of the assembled group is sixty-five and their sexual potency varies from *'in your dreams'* to *'ready, willing and able'.* Not that they ever discuss their present private performances; their current adventures rely mostly on
memories glimpsed through seriously rose tinted spectacles. Not that their current lack of action deters them from explicit comment regarding the way in which they, as individuals, might pleasure the young lady now being somewhat forcefully ridden by a vigorous youth – he was, someone commented, *'hung like a donkey'*; they also observed that she was *'gagging for it.'* The smell of sweat, semen and urine blends unpleasantly with the already foetid atmosphere. The fog of smoke has the perverse effect of being preferable to, as well as mitigating the array natural, human scents.

Before we meet our eponymous character we should spend a little time looking around this room. Put aside for one moment the purpose of this semi-vicarious bacchanalia and concentrate on the room as witness. The bay window, despite the modern double-glazed faux wood, identifies it as a typical fifties semi. This is the front room, living room, lounge, parlour – choose your word: it was formerly used for festive occasions, visitors and

Sundays. The curtains, once eau-de-nil, have now faded to nicotine sludge; a three piece suite in Dralon, patterned with acorns and oak leaves is thread-bare in places, the filthy calico lining shows through. On either side of the fireplace, homemade bookshelves house dusty Penguin paperbacks of various vintages, an ancient copy of the Bible, and at its side, the Complete Works of Shakespeare. The loose carpet, edged by green and brown flecked Marley tiles, is littered with empty cans and bottles; once it was a deep chocolaty brown with geometric patterns in scarlet: it was made by Wilton, expensive when new but now soiled with the detritus of age. The mottled brown tiles of the fire-surround confirm, should there be any doubt, the age of the property and the 2 bar Belling electric fire – square with rounded edges, pinky-red frame - gives testimony to the fact that at some point in the 1960s the chimney was blocked off and the hearth gave way to a cleaner method of heating the room. Over the fireplace hangs a Sun Burst Clock by Metamec, the radials made from alternate spikes of copper and stainless-steel, the digits, dots and minute hands are of stainless-steel, the lone red second-hand ticks gently at the centre. Prints hang on the walls – the Red Skirt, Tretchicoff's 'Lost Orchid' and an ancient chocolate box Constable, in a brown frame. The picture which draws the eye most though is that of Dora: it's black and white, she's about nineteen, wearing a roll-neck sweater, her face is radiant. It is by exploring this picture that we can begin to engage with the scene we first encountered when entering the room.

Do we begin at the end of her life and work back or should we think about her beginnings; their beginnings? However we approach this part of Charlie's story, one thing will be clear: he adored her."